SURPRISE ATTACK

SURPRISE ATTACK

A new adventure in the O'Sullivan's of the
S.A.S. series

by

Leo Kessler

writing as

John Kerrigan

This first world edition published in Great Britain 1996 by
SEVERN HOUSE PUBLISHERS LTD of
9–15 High Street, Sutton, Surrey SM1 1DF.
This first edition published in the USA 1996 by
SEVERN HOUSE PUBLISHERS INC of
595 Madison Avenue, New York, NY 10022.

British Library Cataloguing in Publication Data
Kerrigan, John
  Surprise attack. – (O'Sullivans of the SAS; bk. 2)
  1. English fiction – 20th century
  I. Title II. Kessler, Leo, 1926–
  823.9′14 [F]

  ISBN 0-7278-4946-8

Typeset by Hewer Text Composition Services, Edinburgh.
Printed and bound in Great Britain by
Hartnolls Ltd, Bodmin, Cornwall.

Author's Note

As I have already recorded, when the papers of Major Rory O'Sullivan, DSO, MC (and Bar), *Croix de Guerre avec Palme*, turned up so surprisingly in a Belgian flea market just off Brussels' *Grande Place*, Special Air Service HQ in Hereford was caught completely off guard.* Before the Director of the SAS could react and obtain these priceless papers for the Regiment, they had already been sold.

The 'O'Sullivan Dossier,' as these papers are called by the few military historians who have had privileged access granted them by the current owner) reveal the extraordinary story of how and why the SAS was able to survive after World War Two.

Officially the Regiment was disbanded in the autumn of 1945. However, the strange and intricate events of the winter of 1944, when Colonel 'Paddy' Mayne's 1st SAS Regiment made its bold – and secret – dash through the High Vosges Mountains of Eastern France to spearhead the capture of the key city city of Strasbourg, laid the seeds of the Regiment's survival in the post-war period.

The events of that November in those remote snowbound mountains – that bitter mixture of deceit

* See John Kerrigan: *Kill Rommel* for further details.

and counter-deceit, sadism, raw sex and sheer naked brutality – would ensure that some at least of the Regiment's members would have to exact revenge for the outrages committed then. Then, as ever since, the Regiment took care of its own.

'Strasbourg – Surprise Attack' is not a pleasant story. But, in those days half a century ago, there were few 'pleasant' stories.

John Kerrigan, Colmar, Alsace, December 1995

PART ONE

The Churchill Mission

Chapter One

The damp fog curled in and out of the firs like a silent grey cat. There was no sound save the steady drip-drip from the trees. On both sides of the mountain road the ambushers waited tensely, each man wrapped in a cocoon of his own thoughts and apprehension. Somewhere above them in the murk was the muted drone of a German spotter plane. But that didn't worry the ambushers, the plane would never be able to penetrate the November fog that hung over the high Vosges Mountains this damp cold morning.

Crouched behind the twin Brownings mounted on the rear of the Jeep, Captain Rory O'Sullivan, of the 2nd SAS Regiment, ran over his dispositions once again. He had been doing so ever since they had set up this ambush an hour before. Up ahead at the bend they had stretched a razor-sharp wire at head-height across the road. That would take care of any outriders on motorbikes. Once the enemy convoy was within the ambush area, Taffy Jones, to the rear, would stretch a daisy chain of mines across the road. That would mean the Huns and their French renegade friends of the Vichy *Milice* wouldn't be able to back off once the trap was set. The young red-haired giant nodded his approval. Things seemed to be all tied up suitably. The only thing missing was the enemy.

The minutes ticked by leadenly. Above, the spotter plane had gone, probably heading for the German base at Strasbourg on the Rhine. The pilot had obviously told himself he was wasting his time on a day like this. Rory O'Sullivan looked at the green-glowing dial of his wrist-watch. He wasn't nervous, he'd done this sort of thing time and time again since he had first joined the SAS in the desert in '41, he was just impatient.* Since they had first dropped into France the previous June he had learnt never to run an ambush too long, it wasn't safe. France was full of informers. The locals would soon betray an ambush to the Huns or the *Milice*. Rory puffed out his handsome face in exasperation. "You'd think sometimes," he said to himself, "that the bloody Frogs didn't want to be liberated in the first place."

"Sir!"

He turned immediately. It was Sergeant Smith, the giant ex-Guardsman, who had been one of the founder members of the SAS under David Stirling.

"What is it?" Rory O'Sullivan hissed, blue eyes gleaning as he scented danger.

"Paddy Jones, Boss. He's just signalled they're coming up the mountain road. Listen!"

The two of them cocked their heads to one side, hardly daring to breathe. There it was: the sound of heavy motors labouring their way up the incline to the peak and pass where, unknown to the enemy, the ambush was waiting for them.

Rory acted at once. He whistled softly, once, twice, three times. The handful of tough SAS troopers roused

* See John Kerrigan: *Kill Rommel* for further details.

themselves from their reverie. Behind the twin Vickers on the camouflaged jeep, 'Tashy' Kennedy clicked off the safety catch swiftly and prepared to go into action. 'Tashy' was the Regiment's ladies' man, so known because of his thin Errol Flyn moustache, which looked as if he pencilled it on his upper lip every morning. Rory O'Sullivan nodded his approval. They were a grand bunch of fellas, he told himself. They had been in combat five solid months now, taking casualties all the time, "shooting and scooting," as their CO Paddy Mayne phrased it, but still their nerves were unbroken. They were still game for anything.

"Outriders!" Smith hissed and ducked.

Rory did the same, burying his face in the wet cropped turf. A couple of motor-cyclists were swinging round the corner. They were clad in ankle-length leather coats, Schmeissers slung across their chests, helmeted heads switching from side to side as they looked for any sign of trouble. Rory told himself they didn't know what kind of trouble they were going to run into in exactly one minute. He felt their gaze on the spot where he and Smithie lay.

"Freeze!" he hissed.

Smith needed no warning. He had been through this sort of thing often enough in these past three years. His big body stiffened and he seemed to have stopped breathing altogether.

The bigger of the two Germans muttered something which Rory couldn't hear and then opened his throttle and the two bikes roared on. "Almost pissed in me boot just then," Smithie confessed ruefully.

"*Almost!*" Rory echoed. "*I did!*"

They watched expectantly as the two riders disappeared round the bend. There was a shrill scream of absolute terror. It sent shivers coursing down Rory's spine. He could visualise what was happening up there, as with a sudden clatter the riderless machines crashed to the *pavé* and their motors died away abruptly. The two headless corpses, their necks a thick red goo, would be lying between their jumbled machines, their heads rolling slowly into the ditch like abandoned footballs.

"Here come the rest of 'em, Boss," Smith cut into his thoughts urgently.

Rory forgot the dead outriders. A half-track, packed with SS panzer grenadiers was nosing its way cautiously around the bend. Behind it came a truck driven by a man in the blue uniform of the hated *Milice*. Rory flung a glance around his men. There were only eight of them, including himself and Sergeant Smith and there were at least a dozen grenadiers in the half-track alone. But surprise and speed were on their side. He picked the clumsy-looking signal pistol that lay in the heather at his side and clicked off the safety. The half-track was coming ever closer and in seconds it would be directly in the centre of the trap. Another *Milice* truck was crawling around the bend. Soon, Taffy would be pulling the chain of mines across the road to the rear, boxing the enemy convoy in.

"Here we go!" Rory exclaimed to no one in particular, feeling the old excitement of battle streaming through his big tough body. He raised the pistol. The half-track, filled with bored, sleepy young grenadiers in their camouflaged smocks, was almost upon them. There was no time to be lost. He pressed the trigger.

Plop! Next instant the flare was soaring into the grey sky. It exploded with a slight bang. For an instant he caught a glimpse of the surprised face of one of the German SS grenadiers as he stared at the sky wondering idly what the noise was. Suddenly the young soldier's face was transformed into a strange, unreal, glowing green as the flare ignited. He opened his mouth to shout something. It was the last thing he ever did. In the same instant Tashy pressed the triggers of his twin Vickers K. The round-barrelled machine-guns burst into frenetic activity. Tracer zipped lethally towards the packed half-track. The grenadiers didn't have a chance as the sounds slammed into them. The young grenadier who had been staring at the sky grabbed frantically for his skinny chest as a line of bloody button holes was stitched across his smock. Next moment he slumped down in his seat, dead.

"Christ!" Smith yelled, jumping to his feet and like a gunslinger in a Hollywood Western, swung from left to right, hosing the convoy with bullets from his Sten sub-machine-gun. "Like frigging money for frigging old — " and ducked as a burst of machine-gun fire zipped by him from the back of the *Milice* truck.

"Cheeky!" Rory O'Sullivan yelled above the racket. He pulled the pin of a Type 36 grenade out with his teeth and, grunting, flung it with all his strength at the *Milice* truck. It exploded in a burst of angry-looking yellow flame. The truck bucked like a wild horse being put to the saddle for the first time. Next instant the truck's rear axle shattered and it came to a stop, the machine-gun crew and their Hotchkiss machine-gun thrown to the *pavé*.

Smith didn't hesitate. "Try this on for frigging size!"

he snarled and blasted the stunned *Miliciens* with his Sten. They were flung to all sides at that short range as if propelled by a gigantic fist.

Now the last truck was trying to turn. Desperately the driver slammed his gear into reverse. Tashy, on the twin Vickers, fired a wicked burst at the truck. The windscreen shattered into a gleaming spider's web. With his free hand the frantic, panic-stricken driver smashed the glass free so that he could see. He reversed once more, blood pouring from his hand and then he was heading to the rear.

Smith grinned maliciously as he fitted another magazine to his smoking Sten. Down on the road the survivors of the trapped convoy were trying to crawl to the safety of the ditch on both sides of the mountain road. But the hard-bitten SAS troopers were not inclined to show any mercy for the panic-stricken SS and their French helpers. They had suffered enough in these last few months on the run in German Occupied France. Coolly and calmly, they picked them off as if they were back on a peacetime firing range, taking their time, making every round count.

Then there was a sudden boom and a grey mushroom of smoke started to rise above the embankment beyond the bend. Smith tapped the new magazine to check whether it was secure and shouted above the noise, "Bet that didn't do much good for the Frogs' piles Boss!"

Rory nodded, too busy to answer. One of the SS grenadiers was trying to set up his panzerfaust. He had obviously spotted Tashy in his jeep and was going to try to take him out. He had to act quickly, they couldn't afford to lose Tashy or his jeep. After four months in combat, they were running out of vehicles. He slammed his American carbine into his big muscular right shoulder, squinted down the sight, took first pressure and fired in one and the same movement. The young German flung up his arms as if appealing to God on high for mercy, but on this cruel November day God was not showing mercy. Next moment the panzer grenadier slammed to the ground, blood squirting from beneath his shattered helmet in a thin red rain . . .

After that the heart went out of the survivors and the firing started to ebb away. Finally it was only the odd shot as more and more of the enemy, realising the helplessness of their position, began to throw down their weapons and raise their hands cautiously, as if they knew they ran the risk of being shot out of hand.

Rory O'Sullivan rose to his feet and, cupping his hands round his mouth yelled, "*Cease fire!* . . . *Cease firing!* . . . And Tashy.*"

"Sir," answered a grinning Corporal Kennedy.

"Keep your guns trained on 'em. You can't trust the Frogs."

"Will do, Boss. Though mind yer, their Judies ain't too bad between the sheets."

Despite the tension of the moment, Rory grinned. 'Tashy' was running true to form. As they quipped in the Regiment: "Bring in yer brooms, old Tashy'll frig anything with hair on!"

Slowly the SAS troopers, their faces hard, weapons clutched tightly to their hips, came out of the trees to stare at the carnage: the wrecked smoking trucks; the dead bodies sprawled in the careless attitudes of those

9

done violently to death; the whimpering wounded looking wide-eyed at their wounds, as if they couldn't believe that this was happening to them.

Rory O'Sullivan could see that the fight had gone out of the survivors. They could expect no more trouble from them. He cocked the carbine over his shoulder and said to Sergeant Smith, "OK, Smithie, let's see what was important for them to organise a convoy with a whole platoon of SS to guard it."

"Yes, Boss," the big ex-Guardsman answered. Together they clambered down the bank to where the French and German survivors stared at them, pale-faced and apprehensive. For they knew that in the kind of guerrilla war being fought in the Vosges they might well be shot out of hand. Both sides normally didn't take prisoners.

"All right," Smith commanded. "Move it. *Los . . . allez!*" he jerked his Sten threateningly. Obediently the prisoners stumbled to the centre of the road, hands clasped over their heads, ignoring their dead comrades sprawled out on the cobbles. "*Nix waffen,*" he added. Hastily, the frightened prisoners began to drop their cartridge belts and bayonets as Rory O'Sullivan stared at the bullet-pocked trucks slewed across the road, wondering what they might contain.

A groan from the first of the trucks alerted him to the fact that there was still someone inside it. Instinctively, Smith cocked his Sten, eyes narrowed to slits. Rory nodded his understanding and cocked his own carbine. Purposefully they advanced on the truck from which the pitiful groaning was coming. Again Rory nodded to Sergeant Smith. He raised

10

his carbine as Smith threw back the tarpaulin flap. He stepped forward, carbine at the ready. Abruptly he halted and gasped. Next to him Smith said in a choked voice, "Oh! The poor sods . . . the poor bloody sods . . .!"

Chapter Two

The gigantic frame of Colonel 'Paddy' Mayne of the 1st SAS Regiment seem to sag and shrink as he stood there in the middle of the tented camp staring down at the two corpses in their bloody torn khaki uniforms. Sadly he shook his big head from side to side, as if he couldn't believe the evidence of his own eyes, all the while making little sobbing sounds deep down in his throat.

Behind him the rest of the little regiment stared in solemn silence at the corpses of their comrades, each one asking himself how one human being could have done this terrible thing to another.

Smith cleared his throat. "The Jerries had taken their identification discs away sir," breaking the heavy, brooding silence of the forest camp in a soft voice, as if it were somehow wrong to even speak at this moment. "But the lads have identified the one . . . er . . . without the eyes." He swallowed hard before adding, "By his gold tooth. 'Cheesy' Wright he is – *was*. On account of that gold tooth in the corner. He allus liked to flash it. That's why he was called 'Cheesy'. He joined us in Italy last year."

Numbly, the huge Irishman nodded. "An Ulsterman wasn't he? I remember him now. Couldn't have been more than twenty-one." Mayne shook his big tousled head sadly.

12

"Just nineteen, sir," Smith corrected his CO gently. "He volunteered under age."

Paddy Mayne grunted something and, still not taking his hard, grey eyes off the two mutilated SAS men, said, "And the other poor devil with the smashed in face and . . ." The words faltered away as if he hadn't the strength to finish his words. Or perhaps he didn't even want to mention the terrible mutilation the SAS trooper had suffered at the hands of his French and German captors.

Instinctively, Rory's eyes flashed to the second dead man. They had tried to cover up the gaping wound in his loins where his genitals had once been, but they hadn't been too successful. The front of his khaki trousers was thick with dark red blood. Rory shuddered and rapidly took his gaze away.

Smith cleared his throat again, as if he were finding it very difficult to speak. "New boy, sir. Dropped at the time of the ambush. You remember, Sir?"

Paddy Mayne frowned at the memory. It had been three weeks before, when they had dropped the reinforcements and two more armoured jeeps. The local Maquis hadn't been too keen to fix up the DZ*. Later they found out why. The local Maquis had been working for the Germans and the *Milice*. As soon as the parachutes had started coming down out of the night sky, someone on the fringe of the DZ had yelled, "*Vive la France!*" and immediately firing at the SAS reception party had broken out. It had been then that 'Cheesy' and the reinforcements had been

* Drop Zone.

13

captured. "So we don't even know the poor lad's name, Sergeant?" Paddy queried, biting his bottom lip.

"No, sir," Smith agreed. "'Fraid we don't. But I 'spect he was some poor mother's son, killed before he even fired a shot in anger."

Paddy Mayne's face flushed a sudden angry red. He threw back those enormous shoulders, used to such good effect on the rugby field when he had played for Ireland, and yelled in abrupt fury, "Shoot the bloody lot of them. . . . One by one so that each of the buggers can feel what it's bloody like to be tortured."

"Ay, Boss," the SAS troopers mumbled, staring angrily at the suddenly ashen-faced prisoners. They hadn't understood the order. But Paddy Mayne's gesture made it quite plain to them what was going to happen. A panzer grenadier hung his head and started to sob, his long blond hair falling over his frightened young face. One or two of the *Milice* went down on their knees and raised their hands in the classic pose of supplication, tears streaming down their faces. Another started to pray furiously, hands clasped together reverently.

Scornfully, Paddy Mayne looked at the terrified prisoners. "What a bunch of rats," he declared. "I've half a mind to shoot the buggers personally!"

Rory O'Sullivan nodded his agreement. He felt no sympathy with the men who had tortured his comrades so brutally. He – just like the rest – wanted revenge. All the same, he could guess that their prisoners weren't those who had given the orders to do the dreadful things they had done to 'Cheesy' and the unknown reinforcement. They had to find out who *had* given that order.

14

"Sir," he cut in.

Paddy Mayne swung round, his eyes still blazing with fury, as Sergeant Smith indicated that two troopers should bring out the weeping SS panzer grenadier. "What is it?" he snapped, his mouth working as if it were activated by a tight steel spring.

"I agree with you, sir. Shoot the lot – except one."

"*One*? What d'yer mean?"

"We need one of them to sing . . . spill the beans, sir. Tell us who did this dreadful thing," Rory O'Sullivan answered.

"Got you." Paddy saw his point immediately. "No use trying with the Frogs. They'll blame everything on the Huns. But which Hun?" His eyes narrowed as he stared along the line of terrified prisoners, watching wide-eyed as the two burly troopers pushed the weeping youth against the nearest tree and stepped back. Sten guns already raised.

The two troopers fired. The prisoners jumped, startled. The burst of 9mm slugs ripped the youth's chest apart. He slumped against the tree and then slowly began to slither down it, trailing a smear of bright red blood behind him till he hit the ground, where he collapsed like an untidy heap of blood-stained rags. One of the watching prisoners, a *Milicien* began to scream crazily, jumping up and down like a madman, froth forming on his lips. Next to him, a little man in German uniform bit his fist, as if he might start screaming himself if he didn't. At his flies a damp black patch had begun to spread.

"That one. The German with the 'SD' on his sleeve. He's the most shit scared." 'SD' stood for *Sicherheitsdienst*, the *Wehrmacht's*, security service.

15

"Yes, sir," Rory agreed. "He's just gorn and pissed himself. "Sergeant Smith, bring that little arsehole over here so that he gets a better view of the fun and games. We want him to sing like a little yellow canary!"

"Yes, Boss," Smith snapped. He strode over to the SD man. The German screamed shrilly like a woman and tried to step back. Smith picked him up by the scruff of the neck and carried him, screaming and kicking as if he were a little child to where the two officers were standing. "Now," he admonished, dumping him next to Rory O'Sullivan, "be a good little Jerry and hold yer frigging water."

One by one the Germans and their French allies were shot by the two troopers, while at Rory's side the little German from the SD wept and wept, sobbing like a broken-hearted child, occasionally giving stifled little screams as yet another burst of firing rang out. Then it was finished and the two troopers, sweating with the effort as if it were the height of summer, lowered their smoking Stens and reached hastily for cigarettes with hands that trembled badly.

Paddy Mayne nodded his approval and then ignored the pile of dead bodies, already beginning to stiffen in the November cold. "Sergeant Smith, see that there's an issue of GS rum. The men need it, and send Trooper Rosenblum over, I need an interpreter to deal with this wretch here." He indicated the little German, still sobbing bitterly, as if he would never cease.

Five minutes later Rosenblum, a German Jewish refugee who had volunteered from the Pioneer Corps for the SAS – "When I grow old I don't want to tell my grandkids that during the Big War I shovelled shit in Stoke-on-Trent" – was pressing the frightened prisoner

16

into telling what had happened, while the two officers listened intently, waiting to hear the name of the man who had given the order to torture the prisoners.

Immediately after their capture the two prisoners had been taken by the French *Milice* to St Die on the far side of the Vosges and handed over to the SD for questioning. Apparently, the German commander in Strasbourg, Lt. General Vaterrodt, had wanted to clear the area of Maquis and SAS before the Americans advancing from the West entered the mountains. He had been afraid the insurgents knew too much about German positions and the passes through the Vosges, which would be useful to the Americans and speed up their advance. Mixed Gestapo, SD and *Milice* units had flooded the Vosges, smoking out the Maquis wherever they could find them and terrorizing the villagers into reporting whatever they knew of the SAS. And if terror hadn't worked, money had.

The terrified SD man made the Continental gesture of counting money with his finger and thumb, as if that explained everything, a crooked smile on his thin lips for a brief moment. "Yes," Paddy commented bitterly, "typical frog – knows the value of nothing, but the price of everything, even those poor troopers' lives," and for an instant Rory thought he would strike the smirking German prisoner.

"All right!" Rosenblum snapped finally, "and now the name of the commander of the SD unit which did that to our people – and you'd better sing soon, my friend. I'm getting heartily sick of talking to you." He clapped his hand to his revolver holster significantly.

The little prisoner's Adam's apple went up and down his skinny throat like an express lift. "Barsch," he gasped, eyes wide and fearful, "*Standartenfuhrer* SD Barsch, commanding *Jagdkommado Tod dem Feind.*"

"Hunting Commando Death to the Enemy," Paddy Mayne said thoughtfully when Rosenblum had translated. For a moment he sucked his teeth as he thought over the information. Then he said, "What does he look like, this *Standartenfuhrer* Barsch?"

Rosenblum translated the question and the little man answered a little hesitantly, "He wears glasses . . . and he has got a doctor's title."

"One of those," Paddy commented. "They are always the worse bastards, letting other people do their dirty work for them. Go on."

Again the little prisoner hesitated. "There is nothing much else," he said, "except for his tobacco pouch. He smokes a pipe."

"*Tobacco pouch!*" both Paddy and Rory echoed sharply when Rosenblum had translated, with Paddy adding, "What's so special about that?"

"It's what it's made of."

"Well, what is it made of?" Rosenblum demanded impatiently.

"A human female tit," the little man answered shame-facedly.

"*What?*" Rosenblum exploded and translated quickly.

"A *Jewish* tit," the SD man said, obviously not realising that Rosenblum, who was blond, blue-eyed and very brawny, was Jewish. "And it's still got the nipple on," he added as if it were some sort of achievement. "Whoever managed to preserve it for the *Standartenfuhrer* did a good job by keeping the nipple intact."

Involuntarily, Rosenblum's hand felt to his holster, and Rory O'Sullivan said warningly: "All right, Rosenblum – not yet."

"Yessir," Rosenblum said grimly, through gritted teeth. "Is that it then?" he urged the prisoner.

"Yes I think so."

He fell silent and risked a weak smile at the two officers, as if saying, "Well, I did try, didn't I?"

For a few moments, Paddy Mayne and Rory absorbed the information until Payne said: "So a Colonel in the SD, who has a doctor's title and smokes tobacco out of a pouch made of — " He looked at Rosenblum's dangerous face and didn't finish his sentence. Instead, he said: "Ask him one more question – where is this frigging *Herr Doktor*?" He emphasised the title contemptuously, "Where is he?"

The little man hesitated. Rosenblum again tapped his holster significantly. Hurriedly, the little man said, "Strasbourg, on the Rhine. Dr Barsch always said that in an emergency we could always get across the bridge at Kehl to Germany, where we would be safe."

"Yes, I suppose he would be that kind of coward," Paddy said scornfully after the little man's words had been translated. "With a yellow streak a yard wide down his back."

Rory nodded and asked, "Are you going to let us go after him?"

"You bet your life I am! No Hun bastard is going to torture and kill two of my men like that and get away with it. I'm going to get the sadistic swine if it's last thing I ever do." He reined in his temper and lowered his voice, "Mad Mike," (he meant Brigadier Mike Calvert, the commander of the 1st SAS Brigade), "has suggested we've done enough. He wants us pulled out for a rest and refit. Up to this morning I would have gone along with that recommendation like a shot. The lads have had enough, but not now, Rory."

He looked hard at the younger man with his bold face and shock of flaming red hair.

"I agree."

"We're heading for Strasbourg and this Dr Barsch with or without permission."

In spite of the tension, Rory O'Sullivan grinned. Paddy Mayne was running true to form. He was a law unto himself, as he had always been ever since he had escaped a court martial, for striking his commanding officer, by joining the newly formed SAS in Egypt. "Good show, boss," he said happily. "Bang on!"

The little man was encouraged by the happier looks on the faces of the two English officers. Obviously they were pleased by what he had told them and perhaps he was saved. Hesitantly he forced a little smile, but it didn't last long. Suddenly, Paddy Mayne seemed to become aware of him once more. He nodded to Trooper Rosenblum.

The trooper smiled coldly. "With the greatest of pleasure, boss," he said. Rosenblum crooked a finger at the little German. "*Los, Freund, wir wollen einen kleinen Spaziergang machen.*"*

The little German began to cry.

* "We're going for a little walk, friend."

20

Chapter Three

Seven abreast, the massed bands of the Guards Armoured Division swung by the Arc de Triomphe. At their head, the massive drum major resplendent in red and silver, swung his mace with majestic ease. His eyes were fixed on some far horizon, blind to the miserable world of the half-starved Parisians packed in on both sides, too weary even to applaud.

Churchill, dwarfed by the huge figure of General de Gaulle next to him on the saluting dais, didn't mind. Enjoying himself hugely, he had told himself that four years before the German Army had marched past this same spot and had continued to do so every day right throughout the Occupation. It seemed fitting that they should now be replaced by the Brigade of Guards.

He said, taking the cigar out of his mouth and pointing it at the company of Guards in khaki coming up behind the band: "General, their divisional patch is a shield with an eye in its centre. The Guardsmen say that the eye winks whenever it sees a virgin in Europe." He chuckled hugely, his jowls wobbling. "So far it hasn't winked once. Ha, Ha!"

De Gaulle grunted something which Churchill couldn't understand and glared at the red-coated band, as if he was wondering why as a Frenchman he was allowing the victors of Waterloo to march past Napoleon's tomb.

The giant drum major raised his mace. The music changed from the 'British Grenadiers,' to the 'Marseilles'. De Gaulle's craggy features cracked into a semblance of a smile. Now the crowd of spectators broke their silence. They started to clap in the Continental fashion as de Gaulle raised his gloved hand to his kepi in salute and Churchill, removing his hat, placed it across his chest.

The parade came to a halt. Orders were barked, the officers' breath fogging in the cold November air. The company of soldiers presented arms and then were stood 'at ease', as a white-haired French general started to usher a little girl forward. Her bare knees were pink with cold and her trembling hands held a bouquet of flowers for the British Prime Minister. She obediently allowed herself to be led forward past the soldiers as Churchill smiled encouragingly.

Then it happened. Just as the little girl with the flowers had come level with the raised platform on which the two leaders stood, a civilian dodged out from behind the Arc de Triomphe. Someone in the crowd screamed, another shouted an urgent warning. The civilian was carrying a a machine-gun in his hands!

"Duck!" Churchill yelled, and with surprising speed and agility for a man of his years and bulk, he gave the startled French President a hefty shove. Caught completely off guard, de Gaulle staggered backwards, in the same instant that the civilian pressed the trigger. Slugs flew everywhere.

"Bugger this for a game of soldiers!" but the drum

major's yell ended suddenly as his mouth flooded with blood. His mace clattered to the road. Slowly his knees started to give way beneath him. For one long moment there was an awed silence. De Gaulle, half bent, seemed to be completely mesmerised by what had just happened. Churchill stared around warily, puffing had at his cigar.

Then the dying drum major slammed to the ground with a thud, his medals jingling. That did it! All hell broke loose. Women screamed hysterically, others, terrified, dropped to the ground. Men yelled, "Watch him . . . he'll fire again!"

Gendarmes, shrilling their whistles, ran forward tugging at their holsters.

The little girl with the flowers was knocked over and crushed beneath the feet of the crowd as they panicked when the killer started firing again.

It was then that Guardsman Yates of the 1st Grenadiers won himself the Military Medal and became a footnote in the secret history of World War Two. While his comrades, were still at ease, one arm behind their back, their rifles jutting out in front of them, well-trained guardsmen that were apparently aware of the chaos all around them, he darted forward, Lee Enfield No 4 rifle at the ready.

The killer saw him too late. Guardsman Yates, who had just fought his way up the 'corridor' to the trapped airborne men at Arnhem, had long forgotten all concepts of decency in battle. Now he came round behind the civilian. There was no challenge, no demand to, "Drop that weapon!" Instead, as he had been taught, Guardsman Yates aimed at the broadest spot on his target, the shoulders, and

pressed his trigger. Six well-aimed shots tore the
killer's back apart. At that range Yates couldn't
miss. He could see the lumps of red gore, which
were flesh, flecked with bits of bone gleaming like
polished ivory, flying to left and right. Then the
killer, dead before he hit the ground, fell and Yates,
a boy of 18, said to no one in particular, "Turned
out nice agen." Then as an afterthought, "Sod it,
now I've got to clean my frigging bondhook a bloody
agen . . ."

Guardsman Yates backed out of the big cold reception
room at the Elysée Palace completely bewildered. The
Frog, de Gaulle, had taken the wet Caporal from his
lips, bent down and had kissed him on both cheeks,
saying in his fractured English, "I zank you very
mooch. You are very brave, my boy."

Churchill had offered a cigar, a white five-pound
note and had chortled in high good humour, "Not
every day that a British soldier saves the life of a
French president, my lad! There'll be a gong in it
for you."

The PM had looked at the grim-faced company
sergeant-major, who obviously didn't approve of his
soldiers being kissed by Frenchmen, even if they were
generals and presidents, and said, "Sarnt-Major, give
the boy a three-day pass here. See he gets some special
money from the Regimental Funds. Boy like that
needs more than a kiss to make him happy." Churchill
had winked hugely.

Yates passed through the great gilt and lacquered
doors, saying: "Does he mean I can go and get mesen
a bit o' Frog beaver, Sarnt-Major?" leaving a suddenly

24

worried Churchill alone with the President of the new Fifth Republic.

"Vous avez des problems, Monsieur le President?" Churchill asked in his atrociously accented French.

De Gaulle, who hated to speak English, but thought it better to do so with Churchill, answered gloomily, "Yes, Mister Prime Minister. It is the Communists who just tried to kill the President," he continued, speaking of himself, in that curious manner of his, in the third person. "The Communists are ready for the revolt. They are all armed. Moscow is sending in more arms through Marseilles. The President is worried." He stared out of the big 18th century window, sucking his thick lips.

Now Churchill was worried. Russia was an ally, but already he knew Stalin, the Soviet dictator, in Moscow was beginning to fight a new war against his Western allies, France and Britain. "What is to be done, *mon cher President?"*

De Gaulle shrugged expressively, but said nothing.

Churchill waited a moment and then said, "We can't spare troops from the front to fight a Red revolt in France, you know. Besides the Americans – and they are our masters these days – wouldn't sanction it."

"I know, Mister Prime Minister," de Gaulle agreed and lit yet another of the cigarettes he smoked continuously, glueing it to his bottom lip as he spoke. "The Americans run everything, even my own France so it seems."

Outside, a group of supposed workers was parading by the Palace, crying, "Food for the workers . . . food for the starving workers!"

De Gaulle nodded in the direction of the shouting.

25

"You see, Mr Churchill. They are already working on the populace. Their attempt to take over power won't be long now. But I shall tell you this," De Gaulle's long horse-like face was suddenly animated, "If the Reds revolt in France, the whole Allied front will collapse."

"What do you mean?" Churchill asked sharply.

"The Reds will paralyze the railways and roads. Their usual tactics. That will mean the troops at the front will be cut off from their supplies through Marseilles and Cherbourg, perhaps even Antwerp, if the Belgians join them."

Churchill looked worried. "*Mon Dieu, Monsieur le President*, do you think it would come to that?"

Cigarette still glued to his bottom lip, de Gaulle nodded grimly. Down below, the shouting had given way to angry yells and the sound of blows, as, wielding their white-coloured clubs, the riot police slammed into the mob.

"That attempt at assassination was probably part of their plot," de Gaulle continued, ignoring the sounds from outside coming into the big oputently furnished room. "The Reds will stop at nothing. My spies tell me that the trouble will start long before Christmas. They say the Reds have information that there will trouble at the front by then and the Americans will be in no position to send troops to the rear."

Aghast, Churchill looked at him. "But we have been assured by Eisenhower," the Premier meant the Allied Supreme Commander, "that the Hun was about finished."

De Gaulle gave another of those expressive Gallic

26

shrugs of his, hands raised, palms turned outwards, "It is what my spies tell me, Mister Prime Minister".

Outside, the shouting was dying down and Churchill could hear the curt orders of the riot police as they commanded "*Allez, salaud*! Into the van!" He guessed that they had arrested some of the demonstrators. In French fashion they would be beaten up by the gendarmes in the nearest lock up and then for a small bribe would be released again to carry out more of their dangerous subversion. Churchill sighed under his breath. What a corrupt people the French were, he told himself. Why had the Huns turned out to be such rotters? In the 20th century it would have been much more to the advantage of the British Empire to have been allied with them than the French, who in reality hated the English.

Churchill cleared his throat in that noisy manner of his which he always used when he wanted to attract an audience's attention. De Gaulle looked across at him sharply.

"*Monsieur Le President*," Churchill began, as if he were addressing an audience, "the capture of Paris last August by French troops was a symbolic act, which put the French people behind you and placed you in the position in which you are today. Would you agree that?"

De Gaulle nodded warily, obviously wondering what was coming.

"Now, if you would allow me to say so," Churchill continued, though he told himself with an inner chuckle no one had ever even attempted to stop him saying just whatever he pleased to do so throughout his whole adult life, "you, France, and your government need another symbolic act which would rally the nation behind you and your provisional national government."

De Gaulle looked interested. For days he had been trying to think of some way to stop the Communists before they made their bid for power. What France had in the way of an army was in Alsace fighting under American command and there could be no help from that quarter. At home the Communists controlled the unions and most of the recently stood-down Maquis group. As for the intellectuals, those rats like cross-eyed Jean-Paul Sartre and his lesbian partner, who controlled public opinion, were solidly behind the Reds. As Churchill said, France needed a symbolic act like the liberation of Paris to rally everyone behind the new government, whatever their political creed or class. De Gaulle looked at the pudgy little *'rostbif'* puffing away at that plutocratic cigar of his and said, "Mister Prime Minister, what do you suggest?"

By way of an answer, Churchill waddled over to the large map of France which de Gaulle had had pinned to the priceless 18th century silken wallpaper despite the protests of his major domo.

He took the big double coronna out of his mouth and pointed it at the map: "Strasbourg," he announced simply.

De Gaulle straightened his long, dangling body. "Strasbourg?"

Churchill nodded, looking very pleased with himself. "Yes. That city is a symbol of what the Hun has done to France. Recover it and the Communists will not have a chance. The re-capture of Strasbourg on

28

the Rhine will rank with that of the liberation of Paris. It will ensure that your government will survive this winter, come what may."

De Gaulle thought for a few moments. Finally he spoke. "Mister Prime Minister, General de Gaulle thinks that is an excellent idea."

Back in Africa in 1941 his General Leclerc, commander of the 2nd French Armoured Division, swore an oath at the Oasis of Kufra, in the Libian Desert that one day he he would re-capture Paris *and* Strasbourg. He did so at Paris. De Gaulle shrugged expressively. "But how can Leclerc do so at Strasbourg? He is completely under American command. General Eisenhower wouldn't allow him to do so."

Like a naughty schoolboy, Churchill kept on smiling. He winked hugely and said, "Leave Eisenhower to me. I have the means to make him change his mind, my dear de Gaulle. Never fear. De Gaulle's Leclerc *Deuxieme Division Blindée* will soon be marching on Strasbourg . . .!"

Chapter Four

They lounged in Eisenhower's private quarters in the Petit Trianon outside Versailles. Now it was night and there was no sound save the stolid stamp of the sentries outside on the gravel. Next to the highly ornate tiled 19th century stove, Scottie, her little lap dog, snored contently.

For the last hour the two of them had played bridge. Then, waiting until the orderlies and the Supreme Commander's usual hangers-on had departed, Eisenhower had read one of Zane Grey's cowboy books he favoured, while she had leafed through the week's edition of *Picture Post* and yesterday's *Stars and Stripes*, the US Army newspaper, both equally dull and boring. Now they were alone at last. Eisenhower changed into an old-fashioned striped towelling bath-robe and she had taken off her new second-lieutenant's uniform and replaced it with her latest purchase from the Champs d'Elysée.

Eisenhower whistled softly and ran his hand over his bald head as if smoothing down the brown hair which had long vanished, saying, "Wow, Kay! That's swell!" He ogled her model's figure (for that was what his mistress Kay Summersby had been before the war) which was clearly outlined through the thin black silk. "That kind of gown could make a guy forget even this goddam war!"

"That is exactly why I bought it," she answered, looking at him with her those light-green calculating eyes. "I blew my first month's pay cheque as a second looey on it. I thought," she pouted her lips, as if she were kissing him, "it might make you think of, um, other things." She fluttered her eyelashes.

Eisenhower, who had remained faithful to his 'Mamie' all his married life until he had met Kay as his driver back in 1942, ran his fingers around the collar of his dressing gown as if it were suddenly too tight for him. He licked abruptly dry lips and said hoarsely, "Well, you've done that! I don't think I shall be reading much of *The Sheriff of the Lone Star State* tonight."

"Ike, I hope not," Kay Summersby said and arched her upper body so that her breasts seemed about to burst through the thin material of the gown. "Otherwise I shall have wasted a full month's pay."

Ike laughed and said, "Come on over here, Kay! Get a little closer, willya."

She rose, walking over to him, taking her time, knowing that he was looking through the sheer material at her naked body. She smiled to herself. Eisenhower, in spite of his exaulted rank, was really a small-town boy who thought keeping a mistress was a tremendous adventure. She remembered what Churchill had said to her just before he had flown back to Croydon. "Think of this, Miss Summersby, if you would. In the whole Allied world there are only two people who can influence Eisenhower, and I'm not one of them." He had grinned a little roguishly and rolled the cigar from one side of his mouth to the other. "There is his chief, General Marshall in

31

Washington —", the British Prime Minister paused and the roguish smile vanished – "and *you!*"

She had been flattered.

"That is why we obtained you the job as his chauffeuse when he first came to London," Churchill had continued. "You were to be our eyes and ears at his HQ. We didn't realise just how important you would become to him, for you know better than I do, Miss Summersby, that he doesn't trust his fellow American generals. You are the only person who he can speak to on a personal level. You are the only person in Europe, in fact, to whom he will listen. Now this is what I want you to do . . ."

Now, as she sat at Ike's feet with the Supreme Commander stroking her hair tenderly, she realised just how important she had become. She was not just the ex-model, ex-fire watcher, divorcée who had thought, back in 1942, when the British Secret Service had recruited her that she had made a mess of her young life and was little better than a failure. Instead, she was a woman of power, someone who could influence great events. This night she was going to make Ike change his mind. If it were successful, it would be another step in the direction of that new future that she was planning for herself and Ike.

Back in England at their cottage hideout, just outside Richmond, Ike had sometimes confided in her that he had political ambitions after the war. "After all, Kay," he had said, half-seriously, half-jokingly, "I would not be the first American general to become president of the United States. Wasn't Washington himself a general before he was the president?" She

32

had clung to those words, though she had said nothing to him about it. Ike was bored with his frumpish, middle-aged wife Mamie. What if he divorced Mamie and after a discreet time married her and retired from the Army to run for president? There were already millions of servicemen who would vote for a 'President Ike', with his democratic, no-nonsense manner and ear-to-ear grin. God, she told herself, one day I could be the wife of the President of the United States, if I work at it!

Gently, she took the hand that was stroking her hair and guided it inside the neck of her sheer black gown and placed it firmly on her right breast. Ike shivered with pleasure. "My God, Kay," he said hoarsely as he groped for her nipple, "you're so damned good to me! I've never known anything like this in all my life. Honest!"

She laughed and reached up to kiss him on the lips, her tongue sliding wickedly into his mouth. He shivered again as if he no longer had any control over his body. Greedily, his big square-fingered hand thrust itself down the length of her slim body. Obediently she opened her legs.

He gasped, "Hot dammit, Kay, it's hot and wet! You're just longing for me, aren't you?"

She feigned passion. "I can't wait," she sighed, her body quivering as if in the throes of uncontrolled passion. To herself she said, "Kay, you'll be the First Lady yet!"

Next moment, the Supreme Commander of all the Allied forces in Europe threw himself upon her . . .

*   *   *

33

The SS had caught them completely off guard. After the recent ambush of the SS convoy with the bodies of their two tortured comrades, Paddy Mayne hadn't thought the Germans would react so soon. But they had; they had come filtering through the trees in twos and threes at dawn, hardly making a noise, with none of the harsh commands and shouts which normally heralded a German attack.

Even as the first burst at 50 yards range had ripped across the top of his tent and had awakened a startled Paddy Mayne, he knew this attack wasn't being made by a bunch of kids from some SS training school. These attackers were veterans, they had even tricked the SAS sentries posted to guard the forest camp.

Now he and Rory O'Sullivan crouched behind a rock, listening to the rustles and little movements among the firs as the Germans advanced ever closer, firing controlled bursts to cover themselves, but not wasting ammunition as inexperienced soldiers would have done.

"What's the drill, Boss?" Rory asked, raising his carbine and firing half a magazine at the advancing SS without sighting the weapon. It might help to slow them down.

"The usual drill would be to split up," Paddy answered. "But this time they've got us by the short and curlies. They're coming in from all four sides and listen." He cocked his head to one side. "You hear that noise? They've got some kind of tracked armoured vehicles to support them. We're not getting out of here on foot, that's for certain," he concluded grimly.

To their right, also crouched behind a rock, Sergeant Smith was fitting rifle-grenades to the muzzle of his rifle and was lobbing them into the trees. Perhaps

34

they weren't doing much harm to the advancing Germans, but the exploding grenades, scattering their razor-sharp steel fragments through the firs, were slowing them down.

"Can I suggest something?"

"Suggest away," Paddy Mayne answered airily, though he was clearly worried. They were trapped and he couldn't see a way out without incurring severe casualties and they had suffered losses enough during the last four months. He couldn't risk losing many more men.

"*The Wasp!*" Rory snapped. This was a Bren-gun carrier mounted with a flame-thrower.

"Christ! I'd forgotten about the Wasp," Paddy exclaimed. "But you'd be running a helluva risk. Even getting to the devilish thing will be tricky."

"It's a risk I'm prepared to take, Boss. It might just turn the scales in our fav — " He ducked instinctively as a vicious burst of tracer ripped the length of the rock behind which they sheltered, sending up an flurry of sparks and stone fragments.

"All right then, Rory. We'll give you whatever covering fire we can."

"*One . . . two . . . three,*" Rory O'Sullivan counted off the seconds wordlessly. Suddenly he was up and pelting to the rear, arms working like pistons. The Germans spotted him immediately and slugs stitched an angry pattern at his flying heels. He zig-zagged crazily, praying he wouldn't be hit.

The German firing increased and then suddenly he was in the dead ground where the SS couldn't see him. He staggered to a halt, his breath coming in great hectic gasps.

In front him was the Wasp. The SAS had captured it from the Germans the previous week, but up to now they had found no use for the devilish instrument which was of no use in their 'shoot and scoot' operation. He knew if he could bring the machine into operation the Wasp might just well save what was left of the 1st SAS Regiment.

He sprang into the driver's narrow compartment and pressed the starter, praying that the engine would fire in the damp, cold climate of the forest. It did. Sweet and immediate, the vehicle's engine started to run. He breathed a sigh of relief and swung the gear lever across the grid and into first.

The little tracked vehicle lurched forward and he headed towards where Smith was still firing rifle-grenades from behind his rock. The NCO was the only one of the survivors who knew how to operate the little carrier's awesome weapon, its tracks flinging up mud in a wild brown wake behind it.

"Smithie," he yelled.

The NCO knew immediately what the young officer wanted. He dropped his rifle and vaulted over the side of the carrier in one and the same movement. Now the German attackers had spotted them and slugs howled off the carrier's paper-thin armour. Rory prayed that the engine wouldn't be hit, then they would be sunk.

"Here we go, Smithie," Rory yelled, carried away by the wild, unreasoning blood lust of battle. "Frig the world! Give the Huns a taste of their own medicine!"

Despite the danger, Smith grinned hugely and bellowed above the roar of the engine as the Wasp took the incline, "We'll be frying tonight, Boss, and it won't be frigging cod or haddock!"

36

The little carrier slithered down the other slope, Rory fighting the controls to prevent it from over- turning. Now the SS recognized what was coming towards them. They knew, just as the two SAS men did, what a terrible killing machine this was. From all sides they concentrated their fire on the bucking, jolting little vehicle, as Smith swept the tarpaulin off its frightening weapon and prepared to open fire on the Germans. Slugs howled off the carrier's glacis plate. Time and time again Rory ducked behind the protective shield in front of the driver's compartment as bursts of tracer zipped towards him in lethal fury.

An SS man in a camouflaged jacket attempted to throw a stick grenade at close range. Rory didn't hesitate, driving straight at the SS trooper. The man disappeared screaming beneath the churning tracks. One moment later his severed left arm was bobbing up and down on the track, as if waving goodbye to his panic-stricken comrades.

Behind that terrible weapon, Smith waited no more. He knew their luck couldn't hold out much longer. He pressed the trigger. There was a great hiss like some primeval monster drawing a fiery breath. The cold November air was heated immediately. Then an awesome whoosh, and a searing heat shot out of the clumsy-looking flame-thrower. To the carrier's front the grass shrivelled, hissed and turned a smoking, frightening black.

The young SS men stopped in their tracks. Even at that distance Rory could see the fear in their faces. But there were still one or two of them firing and he pressed the accelerator down and the carrier bumped and bounced its way through the forest.

Smith, standing fully exposed to the tracer zipping lethally through the air, fired once again.

A great red and blue flame shot from the cannon's muzzle and it hissed greedily towards its victims. A bunch of SS men screamed horrifically as the flame wrapped itself around them. The air was suddenly full of the sweet stink of burning human flesh. For a moment Rory couldn't see what had happened to the SS men.

Then the flame and smoke cleared away to leave behind it a group of charred, unrecognisable pygmies, who crouched with branch-like arms upraised, as if they were praying.

Rory felt sick. Hot vomit welled up in his throat and threatened to choke him. The flame-thrower was a terrible weapon, but it was the only way to save what was left of the regiment. Smith knew that, too, and pressed the trigger once again.

Again that great angry roaring rod of fire spurted forward. But the SS had had enough. They broke, fighting and jostling each other in their panic-stricken desire to escape that dreadful, flesh-consuming flame. One was unlucky, stumbling in the same instant that the flame wrapped itself around him. He shrieked and screamed – screams that seemed to go on for ever.

When the flames had cleared, they saw him fused in an upright position, one charred claw of a hand held out in front of him, the burned flesh hanging from it in strips, his face a hideous mess of purple and black blisters, tiny blue flames licking at his legs. Slowly, very slowly, he started to tumble over.

Sickened beyond measure and knowing now that

they were out of danger, Rory shouted above the roar of the carrier's engine, "All right, Smithie – that's enough now!"

"Yes, Boss, I agree," Smithie said in a low voice, his face a sudden sickly yellow as he watched the SS man tumble to the ground. He let go of the weapon and Rory spun the carrier round.

Five minutes later, just as the SAS troopers were hastily packing their equipment into the jeeps and the Wasp, Paddy Mayne had ordered, "We're compromised, we're getting out. I think we've bloody done enough for *la belle France*."

Then Rusty Miller, their signals sergeant, came running across the glade, packed with sweating men, a flimsy in his hand. "Boss! . . . boss," he yelled, "Top priority . . . *in clear, as* well."

Hastily, the big Irishman snatched the signal form from him. Rory waiting impatiently. "It's from Mad Mike," Mayne announced. "Our return to the UK has been cancelled. Here, read it for yourself, Rory." He thrust the paper at the young officer, then hurried away to give out new orders.

The message read: "*Immediate. Proceed HQ Gen. Leclerc 2 AD, Luneville. Mission, highest priority. Orders of PM. Calvert, Brigadier.*"

Rory O'Sullivan whistled softly. He knew that because his own son had been a member of the SAS before the Regiment kicked him out in disgrace, Churchill had always taken a keen interest in the SAS. But this was the first time since he had directed they should capture or kill Rommel back in the desert that he had ever personally ordered a mission for the Regiment. This had to be something big. Then he, too, was running across the glade to get his stuff packed into the Jeep. There was no time to be lost.

Chapter Five

"*Qui va la?*" The challenge caught the leading jeep team completely by surprise. Rory O'Sullivan hit the brakes and the jeep shuddered to a stop half-way down the cobbled road which led to the former ducal palace which was Leclerc's HQ.

Out of the doorways on both sides of the road, two tough-looking French soldiers in US uniform emerged, sub-machine-guns at the ready. Their uniforms were clean and pressed and their faces bore a no-nonsense look. Swiftly, Rory explained who they were and what their mission was while the two sentries listened, not taking their eyes off the jeep team for a minute nor their fingers from the triggers of their weapons. Finally, they were satisfied and waved the little convoy on with a curt "*Allez – vite!*"

They rolled on towards the 18th century palace set in the centre of Luneville. Sitting next to Mayne up front, Rory commented, "Pretty smart for the French, Boss."

Mayne nodded his big head. "Chalk and cheese when you think of those Frogs we fought with in Italy last year. Slack bunch. Most of their officers had served Vichy loyally enough until they realised which way the wind was blowing and then they changed sides pretty damn quick."

Rory nodded and started to slow down as they approached the great gate, guarded by two battle-scarred Sherman tanks, bare metal flanks gleaming silver where they had been hit by German shells. Rory had the uneasy feeling that their progress was being checked by unseen gunners, very itchy fingers on the triggers of the machine-guns.

Still no one barred their way and moments later they were parking in the cobbled court-yard packed with jeeps and other vehicles, efficient-looking staff officers with clip-boards under their arms hurrying back and forth importantly. The whole place had an air of military urgency about it. Mayne could almost feel the tension. There was either a flap on – or an op.

Ignoring the curious glances of the French, who obviously wondered what this scruffy bunch of weather-beaten Englishmen were doing suddenly in their midst, Mayne, followed by Rory O'Sullivan marched towards the entrance. Two sentries presented arms smartly and an elegant young officer in US khaki, but wearing a kepi tilted jauntily on the side of his head, appeared from nowhere, saying in excellent English, "You must be the two English officers we were warned to expect. General Leclerc will see you immediately. Follow me." Without waiting to see whether the two giants would, the French lieutenant turned and began to spring lightly up the great marble stairs, watched coldly by the eyes of some unknown 18th century worthies in their fading portraits.

The young Frenchman marched swiftly down the corridor. Behind the doors that led off to both sides, typewriters clattered, phones jingled and staff officers with bundles of documents beneath their arms came and went hurriedly. Again, Mayne had the impression of a headquarters working all out in preparation for something important. The young officer stopped in front of a highly polished door with a piece of cardboard pinned to it bearing the single word 'Leclerc'. He knocked and almost immediately a hard, clear voice called "*Venez.*"

The officer opened it, snapped smartly to attention and saluted, as did Mayne and O'Sullivan, snapping, "The English officers, *mon general.*"

Mayne and Rory stared at the middle-aged officer with the two stars of a major general on his epaulettes. He was of medium height, perhaps in his late thirties and, above a little moustache, his eyes were hard and penetrating. His tough, brown face relaxed for a moment into a fleeting smile. "Thank you for coming, gentlemen," he said in good if accented English. "Please stand at ease."

The two men did as ordered and Mayne told himself he liked the cut of the French general's jib, though he was not impressed by the major standing behind the general. He was fat, with his belly bulging over his belt. His plump face was damp as if with sweat and he kept running his tongue around his fat lips. No, Mayne told himself, the major looked like those other Frogs he had disliked in Italy the previous year. He wouldn't trust him as far as he could throw him.

"To business, gentlemen," Leclerc cut into his thoughts. The general strode to the big map of Alsace on the wall and positioned himself in front of it. The major advanced and stood at his side, a pad and pencil in his hand.

Leclerc wasted no time. "Nearly four years ago now, gentlemen, at the Oasis of Kufra, I and my men captured the Italian fort of Kufra. It was not an important victory, but a significant one." His words came in short, clipped sentences, with a pause between each phrase as if he were giving his listeners time to absorb the information he was passing to them. "Why? Because it was the first victory that the new French forces – one couldn't call them an army yet – under General de Gaulle had achieved. Indeed I had to use one of my chaplains as a sentry, I was so short of men."

Leclerc smiled fondly at the memory of the giant figure of Father Bronner, with his huge red beard shepherding, out, the terrified, little Italian prisoners. "That day I signalled de Gaulle in London that the Cross of Lorraine was flying over Kufra. I ended my message with, 'We will not rest until the flag of France also flies over Paris and Strasbourg.'"

Paddy Mayne looked puzzled, but said nothing. But the fat staff officer smiled winningly and said in French, "Ah! The celebrated Oath of Kufra. Everyone in France knows about that."

Leclerc ignored the major. It was obvious from the look of disdain on his hard, bronzed face that he didn't like the man.

"Since those days I have kept half of that promise. I was allowed the great honour by our American allies to be the first to drive and capture Paris. Now there still remains Strasbourg."

Again the French general paused and let his words sink in.

"Now, for political reasons which need not concern

44

you, your Mr Churchill and General de Gaulle have convinced the Supreme Commander to allow me to drive for Strasbourg and redeem the second half of that promise."

Mayne flashed Rory a quick look. The latter knew why; if this drive on Strasbourg included the Ist SAS Regiment, then they might well get a chance to settle the score with the mysterious Dr Barsch, who had had the two troopers tortured and murdered in such a sadistic manner.

"I have been told that your 1st SAS Regiment has been operating in the Vosges for two months now, Colonel Mayne."

Paddy nodded, his mind racing at the possibility of new action.

"You know the back roads, the German dispositions and the like?"

Again Paddy nodded.

"*Bon*! Then, Colonel Mayne, I would be grateful to you if you would reconnoitre a route for a two-regimental-strength assault through the High Vosges down to the plain of the Rhine before Strasbourg. Mr Churchill has already ordered your War Office to take the necessary action. What do you say, Colonel Mayne?"

"I consider it a great honour, sir," Paddy Mayne snapped stoutly, his eyes flashing with excitement at the prospect. "My regiment will he proud to lead you to Strasbourg!"

General Leclerc gave another of those fleeting smiles of his. "Thank you. I know of your reputation. I am sure that you will provide my division with the information it needs." For the first time, Leclerc

45

Alsace the High Vosges, November 1944

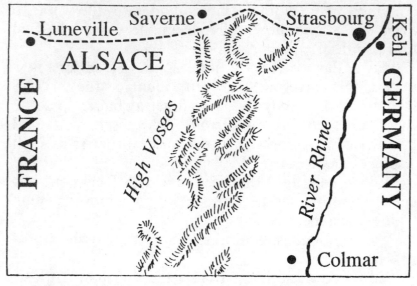

----- Route of the 1st. SAS Regiment

turned to the fat, greasy-looking officer. "This is Commandant Joubert from the 1st French Army." His face revealed his contempt when he spoke, but whether that contempt was directed at Commandant Joubert or the 1st French Army, which was located to the south of Leclerc's division, Mayne didn't know nor much care.

Joubert gave a stiff bow, a little smile on his fat, sensuous lips and Rory thought he looked more like a head-waiter greasing some customer for a large tip than a soldier. *"Je ne peut pas parler anglais —"* Joubert began, but Leclerc cut him off with a curt "Commandant Joubert is here to liaise on a feint to be made by a division of the 1st French Army." Again that look of contempt crossed his face and Rory told himself that there was no love lost between General Leclerc and his fellow countrymen farther south.

"Their 1st Division will push to the Rhine, here" – he pointed to the big map – "in the region of Mulhouse. We hope that this feint will attract the German reserves while my division crosses the High Vosges, which I must tell you have not been crossed from west to east, especially in winter, since the time of the Romans."

He let the information sink in, while the two British officers stared at the big map. Both of them knew from past experience in those mountains just how tough the terrain was. It was going to be no walkover guiding two armoured regiments over that kind of terrain, especially if it started to snow heavily, which could well happen at this time of the year. Besides there were the Germans to contend with, their helpers of the *Milice* and naturally those traitors in both the

French and German-speaking parts of the Vosges, who would betray their own grandmothers for a handful of cigarettes.

Leclerc saw the looks on the faces of the two English giants. "I know, I know," he said hastily. "But if anyone can do it, I am assured it will the gentlemen of the SAS. Besides," he added, perhaps a little slyly, "Isn't your moto – 'He who dares wins'?"

That did it. Mayne beamed hugely and Rory O'Sullivan murmured, "That's right, sir. We'll do our best!"

"You can rely upon us, sir," Mayne added quickly.

"Thank you," Leclerc said. "Now, gentlemen, 26 years ago the French Army marched back into Strasbourg after the Prussians had held it since 1870. I was a boy of 14 then, but I can still remember the thrill of that day. Strasbourg was French again. That was on 22nd November 1918. Gentlemen," he added, iron in his voice now, "I intend that my 2nd Armoured Division will enter the Alsatian capital on that same day this month. So we have little time to prepare for this symbolic act that will rally France behind the cause of General de Gaulle."

He flashed Joubert a look at that moment, for some reason known only to himself, though Rory noticed the fat French major flushed a little at the look. "We have not much time. You have this night to come up with your suggestions. I shall be pleased to hear them tomorrow morning. Here at zero eight hundred hours."

He turned away, the two English officers already forgotten as his mind focused on other things.

For a moment the two SAS men were at a loss what

to do. Then Mayne nudged Rory and they clicked to attention, saluting as they did so and filed out.

The young lieutenant was waiting for them. "I've arranged quarters for your men in the school up the road," he announced, as they proceeded down the stairs. "I am afraid we can't provide those excellent Yorkshire puddings and fish and chips of yours which we ate in Hull*. You will have to make do with our French Army cuisine." He shrugged. "But there will be Mutzig Pils from the Saar for your men."

Rory smiled and told himself they had been eating tinned compo rations for the past four months. Yorkshire pudding and fish and chips belonged to their dreams.

"You will stay here in the Palace with us," the young officer went on.

Mayne shook his head. "No, in my regiment the officers always stay with the men. It's better that way."

He stopped short for he saw that the young Frenchman wasn't listening. "What is it?" he asked.

By way of an answer, he pointed to the fat major they had met in Leclerc's office. Now with his collar pulled up about his ears, almost as if he wished to hide his face, he was hurrying across the courtyard to the gate.

"A strange one, that," he commented, then he dismissed Commandant Joubert and began explaining where their billets lay.

---

* The French Division had been stationed in the Hull area before the invasion.

Chapter Six

Joubert slumped in the chair opposite her, his flies open, revealing his genitals. As always he constantly licked his fat red lips as he watched her doing what he had ordered her to do. Every now and then he broke the heavy silence of the little room with "Open them wider," or "Do it more slowly. You know how long it takes for me to get excited, woman!"

Solange could have killed him there and then. It was a desire that had passed through her young mind often enough ever since the Party had assigned her to the fat pig. But she controlled her rage. This humiliation was the price she was forced to pay for the information that the greasy swine and traitor could give her. So she carried out his instructions, while his greedy gaze followed the every movement of her middle finger, telling herself that Joubert had been a traitor to everyone who had ever put any trust in him.

Before the war he had been in the left-wing Popular Front but all the time he had been passing information about them to the right-wing, Fascist Calougards. During the early war years he had betrayed secrets of the Maginot Line to the Germans. Thereafter he had loyally served Vichy until he had seen which way the wind was blowing and had realised that Germany would lose the war. Hurriedly he had joined the

Resistance, based at some chateau in the Riviera, far from the fighting.

When the French Army had landed there in August he had remembered that he was a reserve officer and had promptly volunteered, only because, Solange knew, he had realised that this was the only way to continue eating well. Now he was betraying that same army. He had been a Judas from the day he had been born.

"You can go a little faster," he broke into her angry thoughts in a husky voice. "I am beginning to become excited." He touched his ugly, flaccid member with a pudgy, manicured hand proudly as if it were a great achievement.

She did as he commanded, groaning a little as if in great ectasy. The sooner she got it over with, the better.

His dark eyes flashed greedily. "You're enjoying, it, aren't you?" he said throatily. "I bet you do it all the time when I am not here, waiting all the time for my great thing to penetrate you down there, *hein*?"

"Yes! Yes!" she gasped, twisting her young head from side to side, as if in the grip of an uncontrollable passion. "I can hardly wait."

"But you must. I am not ready yet," he said.

"*Sale con*," the girl cursed under her breath and continued working her finger in and out, as he had commanded her to do, feeling as cold as ice. Her skinny body was without one spark of lust or passion.

He was holding his 'thing', as he called it, in both hands now. His fat, greasy face was a mixture of lust and what appeared to be anger, as if he was

51

enraged that the 'thing' wasn't stiffening quickly enough.

Then he was ready. "Now you shall have it! Now you'll squirm and plead for mercy, my little whore!" he gasped through gritted teeth. "Prepare to take every little bit of it, *whore!*"

He threw himself upon her. The rumpled brass bed squeaked in protest at his weight. Gasping and puffing, as if he might have a stroke at any moment, he started to pump away at her, while she stared in bored apathy at the dirty cracked ceiling. God, what she wouldn't give for a cigarette, she told herself.

Suddenly his whole fat body trembled. Meaningless sounds came from his gaping mouth. He uttered a cry, as if someone had stuck a sharp knife into him. His spine arched, then he collapsed at her side, gasping as if he had just run a long race.

"*Cochon!*" she cried to herself. The fat, selfish pig never took any precautions. She pushed him away hurriedly; she didn't want a child by a rat like him. She hastened to the bidet in the corner, urinated as fiercely as she could and then washed herself carefully between the legs while Joubert continued to groan and gasp on the sagging bed, his eyes screwed up tightly. Even as she cleaned her body, she told herself she would have her revenge on him one of these days. When Joubert outlived his usefulness, she'd ask the Party for a pistol and personally shoot him in his fat guts and with the greatest of pleasure, feeling as innocent as the day she had left Orange to go the Sorbonne as a country virgin.

Finally he recovered. Still lying on her bed, he did up his flies, saying, "You can't deny you enjoyed that enormously." He gave a chubby-cheeked smirk. "Most women when I've had them will never look at another man. I could tell you stories. . . . *Oh, la, la!*"

"I understand, dear Henri," she said hastily, forcing enthusiasm into her voice "You are wonderful in bed – as always!"

"I know," he answered and looked at her. She wasn't exactly pretty, he told himself, but she was available in a town where there was a shortage of intelligent women who were prepared to play the little games that got him excited. Only educated, intelligent women could do that. Sometimes he thought she might well have worked as an amateur whore in her time in Paris. She seemed to know all the nice sexual tricks despite her mere 20 years.

Five minutes later, puffing at a black-market cigar and drinking good cognac from the same source (after all he felt he had the right to demand black market luxuries as well as her skinny body for the high-level information he passed on). For whom it was intended he didn't know or care, such matters were totally unimportant. The only important thing in this year of 1944 was that he, Henri Joubert, survived the war. Then, he'd worry about the future.

"It's the *rostbifs* who are behind it," Joubert said lazily, as outside it grew darker and the noisy little trams clattered back and forth, bringing the workers from their factories. A platoon of infantry was marching by, chanting the *boudin*. Jobert told himself they had probably been in the Foreign Legion, a bunch of boche no doubt. But Leclerc would recruit anyone to prevent himself and his division being assigned to the 1st French Army in Alsace.

"Why?" she asked, concealing her impatience.

He shrugged. "I have not concerned myself with the matter," he said loftily. "But the *rostbifs* are definitely involved. Earlier this day a bunch of English toughs, looking like a lot of jailbirds, arrived. They are to lead that traitor Leclerc,"* he smirked at the words, "through the passes of the High Vosges. They've apparently been up there now for some two months."

"Where?" she asked sharply.

"Now I wonder where?" he answered, playing her along.

She opened her legs again, revealing the black were of pubic hair. She always knew how to keep the fat swine on the hook. He was the born 'V'. He had probably spent his youth looking through the keyholes of the maids' rooms, she told herself contemptuously.

His smirk broadened. "I see you are hot for me again, my little cabbage, *hein*! But you will have to exercise patience. I am a busy man, you know."

Solange pretended to pout, as if offended. "I'll play with it again," she offered.

"Yes, do that tonight and keep it nice and warm for me when I come again tomorrow. Now what was it you asked?"

"Why are these *rostbifs* here in Luneville and what have they do with that Fascist Leclerc."

He laughed at her use of the word 'Fscist' in connection with General Leclerc, but this time he

* In 1940 Leclerc had been sentenced to death by the Vichy government in absentia for having joined de Gaulle.

54

answered her question directly. "Leclerc has orders from de Gaulle to march on Strasbourg. These English toughs have been loaned to him by Churchill – now there's a real Fascist for you – to help him find a route through the mountains. Now then, there you have it. It is all I know." He looked at the expensive Patek wrist-watch she had obtained for him on the black market, one that he was exceedingly fond of flashing in front of envious fellow officers. "Ah, ah!" he said, finishing off the rest of the cognac with a flourish. "*L'heure bleue* is over. I must get over to the mess before they start dinner."

"You will come tomorrow, same time," she said, a note of fake pleading in her voice.

"Of course." He slipped into his greatcoat, clapped his kepi at the side of his head at a jaunty angle, gave her a perfunctory kiss on her thin cheek and sauntered out, obviously well pleased with himself.

"*Salaud*!" she hissed angrily as the door closed behind him. Hastily she clapped her legs together and pulled her darned chemise well down over her knees, as if she wanted to hide her body.

For a while she sat there motionless in the dying light, not even noticing the coldness of her little room, while outside the first sad, gentle flakes of snow started to drift down.

She could guess why de Gaulle and Leclerc wanted to capture Strasbourg from the Germans. Like everyone else in France she, too, had heard of the Oath of Kufra. The capture of the great city would be a symbolic act that would rally the nation behind de Gaulle. That would be something that the Party wouldn't – couldn't – tolerate. If the Party was going to bring de Gaulle and his government down, it had to be this winter, while the people were half starved and Germany still not defeated. Next year the climate might well be totally unsuited for a take-over by the Party.

Sitting there motionless in the gloom, only half conscious of the noises coming in from outside, she bit her bottom lip like a worried child concentrating on a difficult piece of homework.

Of course, the Party couldn't stop an armoured division some 20,000 men strong, they didn't have the resources for that kind of operation. But what about the *rostbifs*? They must not be too many, the Party's own maquis might well be able to delay or stop them, long enough for the heavy snows to get started in the Vosges. Once it snowed up in the mountains, an armoured division didn't stand a chance of getting through.

Solange made up her mind. Hastily, she pulled on her knickers, threw a scarf around her neck and pulled on her one good coat, made in 1943 from a black market German Army blanket.

Five minutes later she was standing in the softly falling snow, outside the *Lycée des Garcons*, where the SAS were stationed, servicing their Jeeps. She calculated there were about 10 of them, plus a small armoured vehicle. From her own observations she already knew that although Americans rode only three men to a Jeep – they had plenty of the handy little US-made automobiles – Leclerc's *poilus* travelled at four men to a Jeep. Did the *rostbifs* do the same? She didn't know. At all events there weren't too many of them, somewhere between 35 and 50, including the little armoured vehicle. The Party could manage them, she told herself.

Suddenly a *rostbif* in a camouflaged smock came round the corner of the old school playground. He gave her a knowing look and ran his finger along the length of his pencil-slim moustache in the same way she had seen Errol Flynn do it in American movies. He smiled at her and said, *"Bon soir, M'selle!"*

"Bon soir M'sieu," she answered politely enough, but she had had enough of men for this day. She pulled the collar of her blanket coat up to her cheeks, turned and hurried away into the falling snow.

Tashy Kennedy shrugged. "Funny Judy," he said to no one in particular. "Doesn't know what she's missing!" Then he turned and went inside the big, old school. The Boss was going to brief them in 15 minutes and Paddy Mayne didn't take kindly to late-comers.

Chapter Seven

The lead Jeep wound its way along the shell-cratered country road that led to the forward positions of the US 79th Division. On both sides the big, old trees had been stripped bare of their bark by shellfire. Their branches lay in the drainage ditches like sun-dried bones. In the fields to left and right, great brown, fresh shellholes marred the white snow surface like the work of great moles. Here and there a shattered tank, already beginning to rust, lay immobilised, the wooden crosses marking the graves of their crew scattered around them.

They skirted a dead cow lying in the middle of the road, bloated with its own internal gases, its four legs sticking upright. The whole, devasted countryside seemed empty, as if the men of the little SAS convoy were the last ones alive in the world.

"It's always the same," Lieutenant Peters of the 79th's Intelligence Section commented, seemingly able to read the thoughts of his companions in the lead Jeep. "The closer you get to the sharp end, the fewer people there seem to be about."

Paddy Mayne, nodded, but kept his fierce eyes firmly fixed on the ridge-line ahead. That was where the enemy was.

"The 2nd Battalion has got an outpost just right of

that ruined barn at three o'clock. They'll cover us as we go into the forest. With a bit of luck we'll slip through the German line like shit through a goose." His good-humoured face cracked into a smile.

Mayne, who was not particularly fond of Yanks, returned the grin. Peters, he told himself, seemed a good egg.

It had been General Leclerc's idea that they should slip back into the Vosges from the US 79th Division's front. There, the line had been quiet for the past few days; it was thought that the 79th was faced by a second-rate German division which liked to keep it that way.

"Besides," the stern-faced French general had warned them that morning, "there are too many spies and agents in Luneville – *Milice*, German, Reds," he shrugged bitterly and next to him Commandant Joubert had looked very serious, as if he, too, was apprehensive about the threat posed by these agents. "When I move," Leclerc had continued, "I don't want the enemy – enemies is better – to know what I intend. My objective is to leave fast and furious and disappear, with your aid, into the mountains. Let our enemies know what we are about when we reach them."

They slowed down as they approached the barn and a young sergeant with a week's growth of beard and circles under his eyes came out, the 'Cross of Lorraine' patch of the 79th on his shoulder. He didn't salute, as he should have in other circumstances. Rory nodded his approval. Saluting an officer at the front line could draw any lurking sniper to that officer. The NCO knew his stuff.

"How ya doing?" Peters asked casually, as a few

more bearded veterans peered out at them curiously through a shell hole in the wall of the barn.

"Well, nobody's ma has won the golden star this week, sir." He meant the star which American mothers put in their windows when one of their sons has been killed in action.

"Enemy activity?" Peters asked.

"Nah," the bearded sergeant replied, "I think the Krauts have dug in for the winter."

Mayne, eyeing the leaden sky which indicated that more snow might fall soon, asked a little impatiently, "What is the drill now, Peters?"

"This, sir. We've got a Tiger up there, almost in the German —"

"Tiger?" Mayne queried.

"Actually they are the members of our Reconnaissance and Intelligence platoon, but these guys are something special. They all speak German as they wander in and out of the Kraut lines, they are excused all other duties. When they're not on duty they can just sleep all the time and shoot the breeze."

"Yeah," the bearded sergeant muttered and Mayne thought he could trace some bitterness in his tone. "We just about have to wipe their asses for them, the lazy bastards."

Peters smiled softly. "But they do chance getting the chop every time they go out. The Krauts don't take them prisoner when they jump 'em. They just shoot 'em. They know too much."

The sergeant fell silent.

"Anyway," Peters continued, "I've had a Tiger out there, a Kraut really by the name of Dahmen, for nearly 12 hours, poor bastard. He's been listening

60

and checking out the German positions near a trail which your Jeeps can use. Colonel, to get started, I suggest that a couple of us go forward and see what he's got to say. What d'ya think?"

Mayne nodded his approval. He didn't want to commit his whole force just now. That might be too risky at the outset of his mission. He turned to O'Sullivan. "All right, Rory, it's you and me, and you'd better have Smith 175 with you."

"Yes, Boss," Rory replied and got out of the Jeep, followed by the NCO in the second vehicle.

Peters looked puzzled by the use of the word 'Boss' to a superior officer, but he said nothing. Everyone knew the Limeys were crazy as loons. Besides he didn't fancy tangling with the two tough-looking giants who led this little scouting party.

Hastily the Jeeps moved behind the barn so that they were out of sight, while the American and the three SAS men advanced towards the woods on foot. Far away, a machine-gun chattered like an angry wood-pecker, but nothing moved to their front. Not even a breath of air stirred the skeletal branches of the trees. Rory O'Sullivan felt a cold finger of fear trace its icy way down his spine. He grunted angrily and screwing up his eyes peered at the woods, trying to penetrate the green and white gloom of the firs higher up the hill, but he could see nothing.

Just behind him Smith was feeling the same sense of foreboding, for Rory heard him click the safety off his Sten gun. There was indeed a sense of foreboding in the air, but Rory couldn't define what exactly it was.

With Peters in the lead, they entered the forest. He had obviously been here before because he didn't

61

hesitate about the direction they should take. All the same he, too, drew his Colt .45 and cocked it, as if they might expect trouble.

Suddenly, there was a faint noise in the trees to their front. They stopped, hearts beating furiously as they peered in the direction from which the sound had come. The trees rustled again. Whoever was out there was hesitant, as if he didn't quite know where he was. Then the sound stopped. Peters looked at Rory, who shrugged. "Your man?" he mouthed silently.

Now Peters shrugged. "Could be," he mouthed in return.

Rory didn't know quite what to do. Somewhere out there the unknown person had stopped and was lurking among the trees – waiting.

An eternity seemed to pass as they crouched tensely, wondering what to do; whether they should go on. All of them turned their ears to the faint breeze in the hope of catching some sound or movement. But there was nothing. They were apparently alone in the forest, but they knew instinctively that there was someone waiting for them.

Finally Rory gave up. "Let's go on and bugger it!" he hissed under his breath. "They can only shoot us."

"Well," Peters hissed back, "we'll make handsome corpses, Captain!"

Behind them, Smith shook his head and told himself, "Officers, they ain't in this world!"

Mayne said in a hushed voice, "Smithie, cover us. Me and Rory will go first. We're used to this sort of thing, Peters. You follow. All right, Smithie?"

"Yes Boss," the NCO answered, going down on

one knee to present the smallest possible target and levelling his Sten, face hard and set.

In single file, putting their feet down carefully and trying not to make a sound, the three officers advanced, weapons at the ready. There was no sound now coming from the trees. But Rory still felt that unpleasant sensation that there was someone up there, waiting. Was that someone friend or foe?

Rory pushed aside a tall bush, heavy with snow. He saw a little – chapel mainly a weather-beaten figure of the Virgin Mary with a child in her arms, obviously used for prayer by the pious Catholic wood-workers of the Vosges.

"That's the chapel," Peters whispered. Carefully, he raised himself and hissed in German, "*Dahmen, bist du da?*"

There was no answer but the soft rustle of the wind in the trees, followed by a gentle slither as snow fell from their branches.

Peters frowned with exasperation. He repeated his question, this time in English. Behind him, Rory bit his bottom lip, he didn't like their position one bit. If a German patrol happened upon them now, behind their lines, he knew what his and Paddy's fate would be. Any Allied parachutist or commando taken behind the enemy front, even if he was in uniform, would be shot automatically. Hitler had ordered that personally. They ought to get moving and moving soon, he told himself.

"All right," Mayne decided, "we're going forward. We'll find that trail ourselves and then get cracking. Out here like this we can easily get caught with our knickers down!"

63

Peters grinned despite the brooding tension of the place. "Nice turn of phrase, Colonel," he commented.

"Come on," Mayne urged.

Half crouched, the three of them moved forward once more, but not for long. On the other side of the little wayside forest chapel, a dark figure was on its knees, head bowed as if deep in prayer. He was soldier, a startled O'Sullivan could see that, for on the bent head there was a helmet, an American helmet.

"Christ, it's Dahmen!" Peters exclaimed. "What the frig are you doing on yer knees, praying?" he added angrily, because the sudden appearance of the 'Tiger' had startled him.

The 'Tiger' didn't reply.

"What's going on?" Mayne demanded. "What's wrong with the fellow?"

Hastily Peters repeated his question.

Still the kneeling man didn't reply, or even move.

Angrily, Peters advanced a further few paces and grabbed Dahmen roughly by the shoulder.

Suddenly he gasped. Slowly, very slowly, the kneeling man began to topple over, his sightless eyes staring into nothingness. His hands were not clasped in prayer, they were clawed in agony as he had attempted to wrench out the bayonet which had been thrust deep into his chest. Dahmen was dead!

For a moment, the three of them stared aghast at the dead 'Tiger', until Peters broke the heavy tension. "What in Sam Hill's name is going on?" he gasped.

"Yes, what the devil has happened?" Rory agreed.

"I'll tell you what's going on," Mayne said in a very

64

sombre voice. "The poor devil has been stabbed. The question is – *by whom?*"

For a few moments neither of the others was prepared to answer that overwhelming question as they stared down at the crumpled body at their feet. Then Rory said slowly as if he were considering his words very carefully, "That's not a German bayonet that was used to kill the poor devil."

"And it's not an American one," Peters added. "In fact, he's still got his own bayonet in its scabbard."

Mayne puffed out his lips in exasperation, and stared at the long thin bayonet, twice the length of the British 'pig sticker' used on the British Army's standard 'No. Four' rifle. "I'll tell you what nationality it is, if it's any help," he announced grimly.

They stared at him.

"It's a French bayonet. Remember seeing them a lot back in 1939 when I was over here with the BEF."

"But what would a Frenchman be doing stabbing an American soldier? If it was a Frenchman," Peters demanded.

But Mayne had no answer for that overwhelming question, save a moody, "I don't know, but I think we've been rumbled already. Now come on, let's get out of this place. It puts years on me . . ."

PART TWO

Herr Doktor Barsch

Chapter One

"Thanks to your own good self, *Herr Doktor Barsch*," the professor, dressed in the black uniform of the SS beneath his white overall, burbled happily, "we have been able to set up here at the University of Strasbourg one of the world's most outstanding collections of pathological specimens."

His fat face glowing with happiness, eyes sparkling behind his horn-rimmed glasses, he pointed at one of the specimen jars which lined the long corridor. "Look at that, for instance. Could there be a finer example of a degenerate Jewish penis than that? Regard that perfect example of circum—"

Dr Barsch gulped a little and said thickly, "Do you mind if I smoke, *Herr Professor?*"

"Why, of course not," the Professor exclaimed, not noticing that his listeners had changed colour to a delicate shade of white. "Smoke away. Tobacco smoke can't do any harm to these specimens. They'll last for hundreds of years no doubt. And why? Because you were able to deliver them to me straight away from Natzweiler,* almost to order, if I may so." He chuckled heartily, jowls wobbling as he did so. "No waiting around until all those tedious formalities were

---

* Nazi concentration camp in Alsace.

completed to have the body released. Now take that head over there to the left. When I come to write my book, 'A Case Study of Non-Aryan Degenerates and Jews', I shall include a photograph of that head in it. It's priceless! Look at the hooked nose, the typical Jewish thick lips and sloping cranium."

Dr Barsch swallowed hard and taking out his tobacco pouch, which was always good for a joke when he was with his comrades at their *Stammtisch* or a *Bierabend*, crammed the bowl of his pipe with the shag tobacco and lit it hastily.

Next to him, the fat professor of comparative anatomy was still babbling away about his collection. "Of course, when the book is finished I shall dedicate it to our beloved *Reichsführer SS* Himmler. But before then I shall make sure that the Reichsführer is informed of your great contribution to the cause of German science — " He stopped suddenly, the happy grin instantly vanishing from his chubby face.

From far away, the sirens were beginning to wail their urgent warning. The bombers were coming back.

Dr Barsch saw the look of fear and attempted to reasure the professor. "They won't bomb Strasbourg, *Herr Professor*. They wouldn't dare! It would offend the French, though naturally," he added smugly, "the vast majority of the population in the city is solidly pro-German and believes in the German cause." He paused significantly and the Professor looked at Barsch's plump, bespectacled face expectantly. "All the same, *Herr Professor*, there is some justification for having your splendid collection moved across the Rhine to the safety of the Reich. Indeed, that is why I have come to see you this day."

70

"My precious collection must be saved for posterity," the Professor said hurriedly. "How else can I write my book?"

"Yes indeed," Barsch agreed, puffing solemnly at his pipe.

"All those years of research." The fat Professor shook his bald head.

Overhead, the American B-17s thundered to bomb the city's outer forts, while the flak barked, the detonations of the shells making the building shake.

"You see, even those shock waves could damage my collection," the Professor quavered.

Barsch knew it was time now to pose that overwhelming question. "Now, *Herr Professor*, I would gladly sacrifice my time in the noble cause of National Socialist racial science and have my people escort your collection to some safe place in the Black Forest over the river. There are plenty of little villages hidden in the hills which have no military importance whatsoever."

"Would you?"

"Of course, *Herr Professor*, you can rely on me. I would consider it a great honour to help you. However," Barsch paused delicately and coughed, holding his hand to his stained teeth to hide them as he did so in the pedantic manner of the Gymnasium teacher which he had once been, "It would need the permission of *Reichsführer SS* Himmler for me to relinquish my position here." He looked expectantly at the other man.

"Is that all, my dear fellow?" the Professor exclaimed happily. "Why, that should be the easiest thing in the world! I have known dear Heinrich since the days of the 'Struggle'" – referring to the time before Hitler had come to power in 1933. "Indeed, when we are alone together," he added confidentially, "we use the 'thou' to each other."*

He nodded significantly as Barsch said, "When would you try to get his permission, *Herr Professor?*" He swallowed hard, his prominent Adam's apple zipping up and down his scrawny neck, waiting for the other man's answer. He cared not one hoot about the Professor's collection, but he knew Himmler and his like did; such things supported their racial theories, absurd as they were.

What he was concerned about now was his own neck and time was running out. If he could find some valid reason to cross the Rhine into the Reich, he would ensure that he took on a new identity for the time when the Allies invaded Germany. For he was in no doubt that Germany was losing the war. It was only a matter of time before the Reich did and he, for one, didn't want go down with the sinking ship.

The Professor considered him. "Naturally," he said at last, "I shall have to go through channels. I wouldn't likc to use my special privileges to address dear Heinrich directly. But once he becomes aware of the problem, he will act immediately — " He broke off suddenly as a bomb exploded fairly close by.

In its glass case, filled with preservatives, the circumsised Jewish penis wobbled back and forth, stirring the liquid. Hastily, the Professor put a protective arm around the case, his eyes filled with alarm.

* The Professor was referring to the familiar form of address in German used between intimates.

"You see what I mean, *Herr Doktor*!" he exclaimed. "One wrong aiming point by those aerial gangsters and the work of years will be ruined!" He released one pudgy fist and waved it angrily at the ceiling. "Damned Americans!" he snarled. "They haven't one bit of respect for science!"

He calmed himself with difficulty. "Rest assured, I shall start the process of obtaining permission for you from Berlin this very day. In the meantime I will have my assistants begin to pack the specimens. I mean my dear Barsch, how can I allow that beautiful double clubfoot over there or that gypsy vagina, lined with leather, be destroyed by those American *Kulturbolshewiken*? *Es ist unmoglich*!"

Barsch knew he had started the ball rolling. He placed his cap, with its silver skull and crossbones of the SS, on his shaven head and clicked to attention, touching his gloved hand to the polished brim. "I shall be in touch with you every day, Herr Professor," he said.

"How very kind of you, *mein lieber Barsch*, we shall have your permission before this week is out. *Heil Hitler*!" the fat Professor clicked to attention.

"*Heil Hitler*!" Barsch returned the greeting, stamping his booted feet down hard on the polished wooden boards.

Behind him the Jewish penis preserved in formaldehyde wobbled violently and continued to do so as he went down the hall, as if waving him a cheerful goodbye.

Commandant Chretien of the *Milice* was waiting for Barsch in the open tourer, a cynical look on his battered, scarred face as he stared at the civilians

73

crouching in the doorways on both sides, fearfully watching the tiny silver specks that were American bombers.

As usual the *Milice* officer was living up to his favourite motto. "My name may be Christian, but don't believe it. At heart I am an evil, dangerous heathen." Then he would leer unpleasantly at his victim to be. He spotted Barsch and said, "Been delivering a fresh batch of pickled meat to the crazy Prof, eh?"

Barch shook his head. The tough-looking Alsatian, with the livid scar running from ear to ear where once some Communist thug had tried to slit his throat in a street fight before the war, was no respecter of person. Although Barsch was in a way his superior officer, he never addressed him by his rank or his title '*Herr Doktor*', which was to him more important. He was simply Barsch.

The tough-looking *Milice* chauffeur, hung with weapons, including three stick grenades stuck in his belt, opened the door and Barsch slid into the back seat next to the Alsatian. "It was a mission of highest importance and I am afraid secret, so I cannot reveal it even to you, Commandant Chretien."

Chretien took the black cheroot from between his thin, cruel lips and blew out the smoke carelessly so that Barsch had to cough. Inwardly, Chretien chuckled, Barsch was weak. He didn't protest. If someone had done that to him, Chretien would have slapped them across the face, whatever their rank. But Barsch was like many Germans he had met over these past years. They wielded power, but they were frightened of exercising it themselves.

They left the dirty work to others. Barsch was one of those.

He nodded to the driver, the man started up and the big Horch tourer pulled away smoothly and headed towards the city's *petit Paris* area where the clubs and restaurants were, filled even now to overflowing by those who could afford the tremendous black market prices.

"I've got some good news from my informant for you, Barsch," he said, puffing at his cheroot again as the sirens started to sound the 'All clear'.

"Yes?" Barsch said without interest. His mind was concentrating on the Professor's suggestion. He agreed with Chretien that the man was a bumbling old fool, living in an ivory tower, not realising for an instant that his world was tumbling down about him. Still, he had power and, more importantly, connections.

If he could get back across that damned river to Germany officially, then he could take all the time in the world to prepare to take a dive: new identity, new papers, even a new wife. He was sick of Hedwig with her flannel knickers and eternal complaint "Oh, *not again* Hans! You already had it once last month." Since he had first come to France in 1940 with the SD he had become used to younger and more exciting women: women who did things that Hedwig would never have dreamed of doing.

"An informant has given me some really valuable news about the enemy's intentions in Alsace," Chretien was saying. "If we could work on it successfully, we might even be able to change the whole course of the war in France."

The driver changed down as they turned by the cathedral, with its strange single tower. "Ah!" Barsch exclaimed, "We're going to *Chez Sappho*, eh, Chretien?"

Chretien gave an angry sigh. The fat *Herr Doktor* was constantly seeking out new perversions, when he wasn't worrying about his own precious hide. "Yes," he agreed, "We're going to that place. They've got a new show, more of an *exhibition*."

Barsch's eyes lit up behind the thick glasses. "Woman and donkey sort of things, eh?" he asked eagerly.

"Great crap on the Christmas Tree, Barsch!" Chretien exploded. "How would I know! I haven't seen it yet!"

Barsch forgave him the outburst. Soon he would be finished with Chretien and his like. He and his sort were dangerous people. They didn't know when to keep their traps shut. Besides, they were fools. If he had been Chretien, who definitely wouldn't survive the war – for the *Wehrmacht* would abandon him soon, just as they had done his one-time master Marshal Petain – he would have long taken a dive and attempted to get out of France while the going was good. So he said without rancour, "I think we'll see the *exposition* first, Chretien, then we'll talk business."

The other man shrugged carelessly and said, "Just as you wish, Barsch." Then he slumped in the corner, lapsing into a gloomy silence, his face revealing nothing.

Chapter Two

Chez Sappho was packed with German officers from Strasbourg's various army headquarters, all already in various stages of drunkenness. There were prosperous local businessmen, too, fat and greasy for the most part, who had made a rich living off the *Wehrmacht* over these last four years since Alsace had been incorporated into the Reich back in 1940. Mostly they were entertaining dyed blondes half their age, for which they were paying a small fortune in almost worthless marks.

The noise was tremendous. Shouted conversations in German, the local Alsatian dialect, and here and there in French, which had once been the official language of Alsace. Chretien peered through the smoke as the waitress, dressed in a man's dinner jacket and trousers, headed for them. "You want a table next to the floor, *meine Herren?*" she asked in a surprisingly deep voice for such a frail-looking girl. "They cost extra, of course."

Chretien shook his head. "No, one against the wall," he answered.

"But they are all occupied!" she answered.

"We'll see about that," Chretien answered. He shoved the waitress to one side and headed for the rear of the room next to the emergency exit, barging his way carelessly through the throng, once knocking a civilian's glass out of his hand. He didn't apologize.

Chretien had never apologized once in his whole life. He stopped in front of a table at which sat a fat civilian with shreds of *sauerkraut* hanging from his moustache from the *choucroute garnie* which he had just eaten. He had his hand under the skirt of his teenage companion.

The civilian took his hand away and looked up at the tough-looking *Milicien* with the Iron Cross on his chest below the rows of French decorations. "Yes, Commandant?" he asked politely.

"I want this table," Chretien growled.

The civilian seemed about to object, but the teenage whore dug him in his fat ribs warningly. Hastily, he and she rose and left, leaving the table to Chretien and Barsch. He sat down, followed by the German and, crooking his finger at the waitress, growled, "Cognac and no muck either." Then he turned to Barsch and said, "In my profession it's best to have your back to the wall these days, you never know." Automatically, Chretien undid the button of his left tunic pocket and felt the reassurance of the cold steel there. Naturally, he wore his service pistol in the holster on his belt, but Barsch knew he always kept the spare pistol loose, in case he was surprised and couldn't draw the other gun.

"Think ahead Barsch," he had warned the German more than once. "That's how you survive to die of old age in bed with the old woman and warming yer feet on her fat arse." The man had absolutely no culture or manners, Barsch always told himself, but by God he did know how to survive!

There was a sudden, clumsy rattle of the kettledrum from the dance floor. The spectators turned as a slim, very attractive woman in a man's pinstriped suit, complete with felt hat, sprang onto the floor with consciously youthful energy. The crowd started to clap and a drunken major, who Barsch thought was totally out of order, as his tunic was ripped open to the waist, cried, "Take those trousers off, Madame, and show us your knickers!"

The sally was met by drunken laughter from his comrades at the same bottle-littered table.

"*Meine Damen und Herren!*" the woman announced in a deep husky voice "tonight Madame Sappho gives you a spectacle more daring and decadent than you will ever see in Paris or Berlin."

Her words were greeted by a burst of cheering and whistling. She waited until it had finished before announcing "I give you, Henrietta and Hedwig!"

Barsch's mouthed dropped open at the mention of his wife's name. What would she think if she could see him now, in a place like this? He forgot her as suddenly as he had remembered. He rubbed his pince-nez, which he wore in imitation of his master *Reichsführer SS* Himmler, so that he could see the show more clearly, and leaned forward in anticipation. Next to him Chretien did the opposite, smoking his black cheroot with a look of infinite cynicism on his face.

Abruptly, the lights went out. The drunken major simpered in what he took to be a very feminine falsetto, "Hans, please take your hand off my knee, you naughty man!"

Again the crowd laughed but the next moment most of them gasped. A spotlight flicked on, changing from an icy white to a blood red. The light crossed the dance-floor until it came to rest on two women who remained stern-looking and totally motionless there. Both were naked.

Dr Barsch licked his lips.

The older of the two, her thin face hawk-like, imperious and aristocratic-looking, sat bolt upright in a long-backed chair. Behind her the other one, young and beautiful, her slim body powdered a light brown, the nipples of her small breasts tinted pink, waited as if in apprehension.

Barsch swallowed as the room fell silent. Even the drunken major was silenced by the strange sight. What were they about to do, these two disparate women?

The bass drum began to beat stolidly like the throb of a human pulse. Occasionally, the saxophone wailed softly for a moment. The younger woman reached out a slim hand and released the golden band on the other's head and her raven-black dyed hair cascaded to both sides of that hawk-like dissipated face. Using an ivory-and-gilt-backed brush she commenced brushing the older woman's hair, taking her time with long, languid strokes while her small breasts jiggled prettily.

Barsch felt himself growing hot and it was not with the warmth of the room. He twisted his head to one side and ran his finger round inside his collar, which suddenly seemed too tight. Next to him, Chretien turned and stared at the exit door. He thought he had felt a sudden draught from that direction, but there was nothing to be seen. He grunted and lit another cheroot.

Suddenly the younger woman ceased her brushing and disappeared noiselessly out of the circle of red light. The older woman remained motionless in her chair, apparently not noticing the other one's disappearance, but not for long. Slowly she groaned, a groan that seemed to come from deep inside her, and thrust out her breasts voluptuously. Her legs parted slowly to reveal her shaven vulva. At the table, Barsch would have dearly loved to have lit his pipe to calm his tingling nerves. But he was not going to take his eyes off the stage for one moment.

"Paint me!" the older woman said in a hoarse voice.

The girl padded into the circle of light once more. She was carrying a small pot and a brush. Lightly, she dipped the brush into the pot of red paint. The woman in the chair shivered in apparently excited anticipation. She drew in her stomach muscles and threw out her breasts even more, as the girl applied the first streak of brilliant red paint to her left nipple.

"I say!" Barsch said to no one in particular.

The older woman started to tremble slightly. Sweat began to glaze her body. Her breath came in short excited gasps but the girl seemed totally unaware. She continued stolidly with her task, while in the background a gramophone had taken over from the little band. Its music was blatant in its sexuality. The woman started to grind her abdomen and her mouth gaped open in apparent abandon. She was mouthing unintelligible sounds, interspersed with terrible obscenities. Barsch could hardly control himself, he had never seen anything like it.

Now the girl's impassive face revealed a kind of sadistic pleasure. She continued her task, dodging back every time the older woman tried to grab her

81

body. Once she even laughed in a harsh unfeeling manner.

The older woman bared her teeth wildly, hair tumbling about her face. Her stomach went in and out violently as if she were making love. The girl laughed sadistically at her and continued to apply the paint to her nipples. The music rose to a crescendo.

Then it happened.

"Duck!" Chretien yelled urgently and, giving Barsch a push flung himself to the floor as the drunken major yelled, *"Volle Deckung!"* in the same instant that the bomb exploded in a great angry flash of violent red light. Women screamed shrilly. Men cursed. The wounded screamed out. There was another explosion and someone yelled. "There are more of them!" Then the lights came on and Barsch gasped, appalled at the sight of the death and destruction all around. The two naked women were both dead, the younger one sprawled across the other's loins like a naughty child begging a mother's forgiveness. But this 'mother' could provide no forgiveness, her head was gone.

Chretien gave Barsch a hand. "On your feet and out of here. *Los!*" he commanded harshly. "You don't know, there might be more." Hurriedly, he pushed the German through the panicking crowd as outside the sirens wailed and there was the jingle of ambulance bells.

"Oh my God!" Barsch gasped as they got out, pushing their way through the civilians running to see what had happened at the *Chez Sappho*. "What in three devils' names was that, Commandant? A terrorist attack?"

Chretien shook his head firmly. He spat the stump

82

of the cheroot out of his mouth, which he had bitten completely in two in the moment that the bomb had exploded. "No, it's a kind of a warning, and there will be more of them, I am sure."

"A warning?" Barsch echoed somewhat foolishly.

"Yes, a warning that the French are coming back."

"Heaven, arse and cloudburst," Barsch moaned. "So soon. I thought the Vosges would stop them for some while." Miserably, he thought of the Professor's promise. But would he get Himmler's permission in time, that was the question.

Chretien looked at the German contemptuously. He could see just how afraid the other man was. His only concern was to save his own skin, but Barsch hadn't yet realised that there'd be no hiding place for their kind once the Allies won. The only way both of them could save their hides was through a German victory.

Calmly, he said, as the French firemen in their white-painted, old-fashioned helmets started to carry out the first of the dead and badly wounded on stretchers, "The situation has never been better for us personally and for Germany since the Invasion back in June."

Barsch looked at him as if he had suddenly gone crazy. "How do you mean?"

Chretien gave him the benefit of his cold, cruel smile. "As you know, Barsch, I have my finger in several different pies. It is wise to do so if one is to survive in our line of business."

"Yes, yes go on," Barsch said eagerly.

"My informant tells me that the Communists will try to bring down de Gaulle's government before

83

Christmas. And you know what that will mean for the front?"

"Yes," Barsch said a little hesitantly.

They were bringing out the naked older woman, a blood-stained towel over where her head had been. Automatically, Barsch noted that that not only had her hair been dyed raven black, but her pubic hair had been so, too. It had been shaven into a precise 'V', which could been seen through the powdered stubble.

"Well what?" Chretien demanded urgently, coming back to the question.

"Well, the transport system would be paralysed – roads, rail and ports. There'd be no supplies reaching the enemy's front."

Chretien nodded. "Exactly. More even. The factories supplying the enemy, the workshops repairing their tanks and other vehicles would down tools. My informant tells me that part of the French Army, still in training, would be prepared to go on strike too. They live like pigs in American cast-offs and with piss-poor food. De Gaulle's government would topple in one week flat."

"But would the Allies send in troops?" Barsch objected.

"Where would they find sufficient troops to pacify the whole of France?" Chretien said scornfully. "But there is one fly in the ointment."

"And what's that?" asked Barach.

"Leclerc and his armoured division are to attempt to take Strasbourg in a surprise attack, that's what my informant tells me. "That was what that bomb was about – and there'll be others. It's a warning. If Leclerc takes Strasbourg there will be no revolution."

"But what can we do about it?" Barsch asked. "We're just a handful of police officials and *Milice*." He looked expectantly at the other man. They were bringing out the owner, the woman dressed as a man. She was moaning miserably and trying to cover her loins. The reason was obvious – 'she' was really a man. That was only too visible.

Chretien gave that tough cynical laugh of his. "Nothing is what it seems, eh Barsch? What can we do about it?" He echoed the German's question.

"I shall tell you. Somehow or other we shall hinder the start of Leclerc's attack. If we can do so until the snows come in the High Vosges, he won't have a cat's chance in hell of getting through the mountains to Strasbourg." He looked pointedly at the other man, "And let me finish on this, Barsch. If the Americans can't supply the front because of the revolution in de Gaulle's France, *then Germany might still win the war in the West!*"

Chapter Three

It had been a good day for what was left of the 1st SAS Regiment. Despite that mysterious killing of Peters' 'Tiger' nothing else had happened. They had found the trail Peters had mentioned and its surface had been strong enough to bear tanks. "After a couple of hours of Leclerc's Shermans passing over it, it'll probably be a sea of mud," Paddy Mayne had maintained.

"But that will be long enough."

The trail had led them to a small country road winding up into the mountains. Once, they had passed through a small village, but it was deserted. They soon found out why. The villagers were all busy in the local cemetery some way out, planting red candles on the graves of the dead and generally tidying up the tombs. Rory had exclaimed, "Of course, it's All Hallows. A big day for Catholics."

"Damned Papists!" Mayne had snorted. "Bunch of superstitious fish-eaters." He had stared at the villagers as the soldiers had rolled past in their jeep, but they were apparently too engrossed in their self-appointed tasks to notice the SAS men. Perhaps they had seen enough troops over these past four years.

Rory O'Sullivan, the lapsed Catholic, had not been offended by the giant Ulsterman's comment. He was used to it by now. He said, "One thing is clear. We must be through the Jerry front-line now, otherwise I don't think they would have ventured to the church-yard, if there were any chance of fighting."

"'Spect you're right," Mayne had agreed and ordered their signaller, blond, handsome young Corporal Stevens, who had already won the Military Medal and Bar, to report back to Leclerc's HQ.

But as the day wore on, it was becoming increasingly cold and the snow flurries started to be more frequent. In the open jeeps, the SAS troopers buddled down in their seats, trying to keep out of the wind. But it was virtually impossible and the men became increasingly red-faced and bleary-eyed as the razor-sharp snow-flakes bit into their skin like knives.

Tough as they were, Mayne knew that he couldn't keep them out in the open at this altitude much longer. They needed a roof over their heads and warm food this night.

By three, Mayne, too, had had enough. Only an hour before the little convoy had stopped and had brewed up, but even the mug of 'sar'nt-major's char' – a thick brown liquid enriched with creamy Carnation milk – had not warmed their frozen bodies for more than a few minutes or so. It was time to find cover for the night.

Ten minutes later they turned a bend in the mountain road and spotted the first house they had seen since they had passed the little village. Mayne ordered the lead jeep to stop and he and Rory surveyed the place through their binoculars.

It was a typical farmhouse of the area: a half-timbered, partially white-washed structure, housing both humans and animals under the same roof. There were no signs of humans in the flagged yard and, at this time of the year, the animals would be in their stalls. But the great pile of steaming brown manure, under the kitchen window, indicated that there were plenty of them somewhere in the place.

"God, how can they stand the pong right under the kitchen window?" Rory commented as he lowered his glasses.

"It's a way of showing off your wealth, you dunderhead, Rory," said Mayne. "The more cow shit you've got under yer window, the richer you are." He sighed and rubbed his right ear, which was completely numb with cold. "What do you think?"

"Do you want me and Smithie to have a look-see before we all go in?"

"Yes, I think that's best," Mayne agreed. "But I'm praying everything's OK. We need to get the chaps under cover before the snow really starts." He indicated the leaden sky, looking threatening and ominous.

Five minutes later, Smith and Rory O'Sullivan crept through the trees to the right of the lonely farmhouse. "Looks to me, Boss," Smith whispered as they advanced almost noiselessly, "as if they're too poor to have a pot to piss in. But there's somebody at home all right. Look at the smoke coming from yon chimney."

Rory nodded. He'd seen it too. He shivered dramatically at the thought of getting out of the freezing cold and being able to warm himself in front of a roaring fire. For there were trees a plenty for fuel and he could smell that old familiar homely scent of wood smoke. "Standard Operating Procedure," he announced as they came parallel with the rundown mountain farm. "I'll do the door. You cover me."

"Got it, Boss," Smith snapped, the biting cold forgotten now. He snapped the safety off his Sten gun and cocked it carefully. Rory went forward, walking on the sides of his boots to make the least possible noise on the cobbled yard. He reached the door. It was weatherbeaten and looked as if it hadn't been painted ever since the house was built in 1756, as the date carved into the lintel indicated.

Once, Rory had been somewhat hesitant of going through other people's front doors. It hadn't seem quite proper but not any longer. Closed doors and waiting outside spelled sudden death in his book. He nodded to Smith, who nodded back, grasped the handle and flung it open. His nostrils were assailed by the smell of stale apples, manure, sweat and ancient misery, but he had no time for the smell. His eyes were fixed on the old crone at the end of the dark, flagged corridor which led to the heart of the farm. She was bent over a twig broom, stirring the dust. For a moment she didn't hear him – she was obviously deaf – but she did feel the sudden icy draught.

Her head creaked round towards the door. Suddenly she gasped as she saw the young giant standing there, pistol in his hand. She dropped the besom and next instant threw her dark ankle-length apron up over her incredibly wrinkled, ancient face, as if she were wanting to blot out a particularly horrible bad dream.

Rory laughed softly. They were OK. He whistled to Smith. Outside, the sergeant put his hand, fingers outspread, to the centre of his head so that Mayne, watching through his binoculars, could see the gesture clearly. It was the infantry signal for 'Rally on me.'

Mayne didn't hesitate. He snapped out an order. Gratefully the freezing drivers started up their motors and Corporal Stevens, whose nose was red with cold and sporting an opaque dewdrop, commented, "Thank Gawd for that. It's bloody parky! I think my thing has frozen up and dropped off."

"Get on with it," Tashy Kennedy, his running mate, who had always been slightly envious of the other man's blond good looks, snorted. "Pull the other one, Stevie, it's got frigging bells on. That thing o' yourn'll never drop off. They'll have to dynamite it first!"

Five minutes later the jeeps were drawn up behind the animal part of the farm, sentries had been posted (undercover for once) and Mayne was stalking into the big kitchen, from the roof of which hung dusty hams and a great thick smoked sausage, to view the farmer and his family, who Rory and Smith had lined up.

"We must have crossed the linguistic frontier," Rory explained, as Mayne eyed the farmer, a tall surly-looking man who had lost his right hand and had had it replaced with a wooden one in a brown leather glove. "These are German-speakers."

Mayne nodded and took in the photograph on the wall behind the civilians which showed a soldier, very much like the farmer, in *Wehrmacht* uniform. Had he lost that hand fighting in the German Army, he wondered. Aloud he said, "Any arms?"

"Just a 12-bore shotgun," Rory answered. "The best I could understand – they speak a terrible German dialect – he uses it for hunting in the season."

Mayne nodded his understanding and looked along

the line of apprehensive civilians, the old half-daft granny, the farmer's wife, with hands like a Belfast bricklayer, and the two teenage children, who stared back at him in surly fashion. But then, Mayne told himself, peasants all over the world always looked surly and suspicious. "Is that the lot?" he asked. "Plus the maid?"

Rory nodded. "We searched the place pretty thoroughly. That's all we could find – plus the maid."

"Where's she?"

"In the larder. The old boy didn't like it," he indicated the farmer. "But she's rustling up some vittels so that the womenfolk can cook the lads a nice hot stew. Put the lead back in their pencils."

"You can say that again, boss," Tashy Kennedy said heartily, his mind full of Fifi the French Maid, all suspenders, black silk stockings and short skirts. "I only wished I had somebody to write to."

Mayne, who was a bit of a moralist, froze the corporal with a hard look, before saying, "Good show, Rory. Just the job." He turned to Stevens and commanded, "Get on the wireless and report our position to Leclerc's HQ. Might be useful to the General later."

Now, as the frozen troopers crowded round the roaring open fire, the logs crackling merrily, the farmer's wife and the old crone set up a huge cauldron of water, cutting into it *speck*, the hard smoked bacon of the area, and great slices of air-dried sausage, shouting in their incomprehensible dialect at the maid still busy in the pantry, finding whatever was needed for the stew.

Behind them on the great board kitchen-table, Paddy worked out the map references for a waiting

91

Stevens who had earphones clamped to his head, ready to send to Leclerc's headquarters in Luneville. Outside the wind howled and the first flurries of snow beat angrily against the little window panes.

Rory, for his part, took a rest. He was enjoying the break in the warm kitchen, beginning to savour the first smells of the cooking. It was like being back at one of the great, tumbledown houses of the O'Sullivans before the war, after a day's hunting.

Upstairs, the adults would be enjoying their whiskies and GT's, while he was placed in the kitchen with the maids and cooks fussing over 'Master Rory,' bringing him cups of hot, steaming tea and great chunks of hot, freshly baked bread, dripping with home-made butter. Despite the fact that they were miles behind the enemy's lines, he felt warm, snug and safe in this homely remote farmhouse kitchen. He yawned and wished he could fall asleep. But somehow he couldn't. For a while he pondered why not, his eyes closing all the time.

Then it struck him. It was the farmer, slumped in a chair at the far end of the kitchen, his haggard face set in a look of sullen resentment as his eyes flashed from the women busy at the fire to the soldiers smoking quietly and enjoying this time out of war, chatting softly to one another.

Rory looked at the Alsatian through veiled eyes, trying to figure out what was going through his mind, but in the end he gave up just as the maid came through the door, carrying a huge basket of vegetables.

"Who's that?" Paddy Mayne demanded, alert instantly.

"Just the maid, sir," Rory replied, sitting up.

At the mention of "maid", Tashy Kennedy turned sharply, mind full of those black silk stockings and frilly knickers. His mouth fell open stupidly.

This maid was a great buxom wench, with breasts bursting through her patched blouse, her feet clad in wooden shoes, her sturdy legs clothed in dark woollen stockings. As he confided to his running mate Stevens later, "She ain't, no Fifi the French maid, old mate. But did yer see them pair of lungs on her! I could get my head between them tits and not hear a thing for 48 hours, old cock."

At the door *Rottenführer* Schreiber of the Hitler Youth, the farmer's son, heard only too well. Ever since the Maquis had come into the mountains back in 1943, mostly "bandits" as his father called them, looting and stealing from good honest farmers, they had had contact with Commandant Chretien's *Milice*.

The Commandant had always paid well for information, not in worthless marks or francs, but in good solid silver, which would still be of value after the war. As his father had maintained, "Nobody looks after farmers. You sow seed in March which might or might not come up in June. If it don't, who cares? Farmers have got to look after themselves. Silver under the bed, that's our insurance for the future, my boy. Blood money some people might call it, but not we farmers."

Now the young boy with the same shifty eyes as his father knew exactly what he had to do. He had seen enough. What he knew would be worth a good few silver pre-war francs to Commandant Chretien. He turned and, tucking his collar up to protect his face, trudged into the falling snow. Moments later he disappeared into the howling white gale.

Chapter Four

"*L'heure bleue*," Commandant Joubert said jauntily, as she opened the door and saw the fat swine standing there, knocking the snow off his kepi. He was very flushed and his breath smelled. He had been drinking, she could see that plainly and the pig was always worse when he had been drinking. Outside, the snow still pelted down, but there wasn't enough yet to stop Leclerc in the mountains. Today she'd use Joubert to find out when the 2nd French Armoured Division was due to set off its race for Strasbourg. Control urgently needed to know that date.

She forced a winning smile and said, "Please come in *cherie*. I've been longing for it all this long dreary day."

"Good," he said and squeezed her left breast hard. It hurt, but her pinched, pale face revealed nothing. "I've brought a friend with me. We've just had a few drinks and decided on a day like this with three of us it might be more fun." He licked his fat red lips.

"But," she began in sudden alarm.

"Don't worry," he interrupted her. "It's not another man." He turned and called down the dingy stairs, "It's all right, Colette, you may come up. The coast is clear." He beamed at what he thought was a joke.

There was the sound of heavy shoes ascending the

94

creaking stairs, as the girl wondered who the fat swine had brought with him. What kind of woman had he brought with him? A moment later she found out.

"Captaine Colette Colbert," Joubert said with a flourish, extending his right hand like a head waiter bowing to the best table an honoured guest who tipped well.

"*Bon jour*," the big woman in the uniform of a French Army captain said and extended her hand.

Hesitantly, Solange took it and felt her own hand being squeezed very hard. But that wasn't all. The big women with the horsey face and suspicion of a moustache pressed her bent middle finger into the palm of her hand and Solange knew what that signified.

As Joubert helped the Captain out of her greatcoat to reveal her dumpy figure, with a massive bosom straining at the buttons of her tunic, Solange's brain raced. What was she to do? God, how the fat swine always humiliated her!

The Captain sat down and studied her with her dark calculating eyes, while Joubert explained that Captain Colbert had just been posted to his office from the 1st Army. "Though, of course, I knew her before when I served with the 1st. We became good friends, didn't we, my dear Colette – *in our own fashion*," he emphasized the words.

The woman grunted something, but didn't take her eyes off the girl for one moment. It was as if she were sizing her up carefully. For what reason, Solange could only guess.

Joubert sat down and produced a half-full bottle of brandy from his greatcoat. "Get some glasses, my dear. We might as well finish this before the fun and games commence." He leered at her, but beside him on the sofa the big woman's expression didn't change. "It'll get us in the right mood, *hein*."

Reluctantly, Solange fetched the glasses from behind the curtain which screened off her 'kitchen', a gas ring and a sink. Joubert poured generous portions into each glass, handing her the biggest, with "That'll warm you up, my little cabbage." He winked knowingly and licked his fat lips once more before raising his glass in toast, "*Salut!*"

"*Salut!*" the big captain said and Solange heard herself saying the same word though she had never felt less like toasting somebody. She was frightened, trapped, disgusted. What the devil was she going to do?

Joubert did all the talking. His dark eyes flashed and he gesticulated often with his pudgy hands as he did so. She realised that he was drunker than she had thought. And all the while the big woman stared and stared at her, no expression on her face, her features set and hard. Solange began to feel really afraid.

Outside, nothing could be seen. The snow was falling down as if it would never cease. It was a total white-out. Sitting there, feeling so very trapped, she wondered if she could get away with telling him that she had her period and that she wasn't capable of performing. But even as she thought about it, she knew it wouldn't work. Joubert would find some other perverted way of satisfying his lust.

Suddenly the big woman finished her drink with a flourish and spoke for the first time since she had been introduced. "I think it is about time to start, Joubert," she growled in that deep voice of hers.

Joubert's pudgy hand dropped to his flies. "Well, let

the fun and games commence," he said drunkenly. "I think all of us are in the right mood." He winked at the big woman.

Her face remained stern and she didn't return the knowing wink. Instead she said, "Is there somewhere where I can get ready?"

"Get ready?" Solange echoed, her eyes flashing from one face to the other. "How do you mean, get ready?" Anger was beginning to replace her initial fear now. What right had they to make such demands upon her?

Joubert answered the woman's question for her. "There's the lavatory," he indicated the door with his glass. "In there." He licked his fat, red lips yet again and they gleamed wetly.

The woman rose and picked up her khaki sling bag. She went into the lavatory, closing the door carefully behind her. Joubert rubbed his flies happily. "I think we're all going to enjoy this," he said and leaned back, making himself more comfortable for what was to come.

"What is she going to do?" asked Solange, backing towards the 'kitchen'.

"Wait and see," Joubert answered. "I wager this is going to be an experience you will enjoy a great deal. I expect you'll be begging for more of it in the future. Let her do what she likes. It will be better that way." Suddenly he was stuttering, as if the excitement was becoming too much for him. "Captain C-C-Colbert can be quite nasty if th-things don't go her w-way."

Solange put her hand behind her back and thrust it through the curtain, while Joubert settled in the chair, already undoing his flies. She saw that he was already

97

bulging down there and the sight horrified her. Usually he was so slow at getting excited, he was virtually impotent. So the woman was going to do something very special if could get that excited so soon. Her hand felt what she sought. She grabbed it and felt the hate well up inside her like a burning fire.

"She'll undress you and tell you what to do," Joubert was saying, as the door to the lavatory opened. "She likes giving orders, and having them obeyed." He stopped short, his fat mouth dropping open stupidly. "My . . . G-G-God," he stuttered. "Oh . . . my God!"

The big woman stood there, totally naked save her flat sensibly heeled Army shoes. She had painted a large moustache on her upper lip and at any other time Solange would have found her totally ludicrous, an absolute figure of fun, save for what now was tied to her ample waist.

Solange stared at it in horror: a great leather rod, which protruded far beyond the woman's ample stomach, wobbling threateningly with every breath she took.

The big woman seemed to like the look of fear in the skinny girl's eyes, for she said in a soothing voice, "Do not be afraid. I shall be gentle with you, girl." With her free hand she ran her fingers along the length of the absurd, painted-on moustache like a man might do. Then she began to advance on the horrified girl, the leather monstrosity bouncing up and down menacingly, her eyes gleaming with cruel lust.

"No!" Solange yelped. "I won't do it!"

"You'll enjoy it, my darling," Joubert breathed, his flies open now, busy with himself as watched the spectacle, entranced. "She'll . . . look after you all right!"

Now the big woman was almost upon her. Solange could smell the stale odour of someone who sweated profusely. She was repelled, nauseated. The big woman stretched out her free hand, the nails bitten to the quick, the fingers brown with tobacco stains. "I want you," she demanded in that husky voice of hers. "Let's have no more of this fuss, girl. You'll have to accept it – all of it – sooner or later. So we mustn't play around."

"Yes, yes!" Joubert cried, carried away with the sheer sexual excitement of the scene before his eyes in this dingy working-class room. "You'll h-h-have to take it. A-a-all of it!"

The woman reached for Solange's breast.

Suddenly, amazingly, something snapped inside the skinny little girl. The Party, her role as its spy, everything was forgotten as a feeling of sheer naked revulsion swept through her. "You dirty pigs!" she cried, her pale face abruptly flushed with anger. Naked hatred blazed from her eyes.

"Don't be silly — " the woman stopped short and gasped when she saw what had appeared in Solange's hand, as if by magic.

Solange raised the long, gleaming kitchen knife, eyes blazing furiously. "Not a step further, *bitch!*" she hissed, spittle flying from her lips.

"Don't be a little fool," Joubert cried. "Look, you're spoiling my pleasure!"

The comment made her angrier still. It was typical of him and all the decadent French bourgeoisie who had run the country for so long. They thought everything and everybody in France was there for *their* pleasure, and when things got ruined or broken it was up to the common people to pick up the pieces.

"*Sale con!*" she spat at him, not taking her gaze off the big woman, who was now obviously puzzled and undecided.

"Don't you dare talk to me like that!" Joubert snapped, buttoning up his flies. "Don't forget I know all about you."

"And I know all about you," she shot back. "You're an evil lecher. A triple traitor. A rat who would sell his own mother for a sou."

"Well, I'll be damned!" Joubert exclaimed. He rose to his feet, but he had forgotten, in his sudden rage, to buckle his belt. Absurdly his trousers slipped down to his fat pale knees. He stumbled and fell forwards. Next instant he screamed, high, like a woman might, as the long blade of the kitchen knife sliced into his fat stomach.

Solange let go of the hilt and Joubert staggered back, the knife still protruding from his belly, his pudgy hands getting weaker by the second trying to pluck that killing blade from his intestines. To no avail. He fell backswards, moaned once, then his head rolled to one side and he was dead.

"*God Almighty,*" the big woman cried aghast, sex forgotten. "You've killed him!" she exclaimed. "He's dead — " She stared at the pale-faced, skinny girl, as if seeing her for the first time. "Why, you murderess!" Then hastily, remembering her own compromised position, she started fumbling with the leather straps of the artifical penis, crying to herself, "Oh! Come on, *come on.* What a scandal!" while Solange stared at her as if mesmerised, knowing already that she was doomed.

Chapter Five

General Leclerc took his time with the prisoner. He was courteous as well as patient, even though, when she had been pushed into his office by the gendarmes who had arrested her, she had clenched her fist and cried, "Power to the people! Long live the people's revolution!" He had, as an aristocratic, devout Catholic, always hated Communists, but he had always admired bravery and defiance in people who were in a hopeless situation, and this pale, skinny girl *was* in exactly that kind of situation. It would be the guillotine for her. This winter, de Gaulle was merciless with his enemies.

Gravely, he had listened to the evidence of the female captain, who was most obviously a predatory lesbian of the absolutely worse kind: the sort who would seduce virginal schoolgirls and ruin them for life. For him that was the worse type of sexual deviance. Women, in his strict Catholic mind, were born to have babies. Her kind never would.

Now, as the snow came hissing down outside, blanketing out what little remained of the afternoon light, he looked at her and asked her again: "Were you an agent of the French Communist Party?" adding quickly as if not to alarm her, "That, I must explain, is not a crime in itself, *M'selle*."

Numbly, she nodded.

He absorbed the information for a moment, staring at the big woman, who did not return his look, as if she were fearful to do so, before turning back to the girl in the chair and saying, "Was it your task to obtain information from Commandant Joubert?"

Again she nodded wordlessly.

"What kind of information did you get from him and how did you reward him? Sexually?"

"Yes," she said in a small voice.

The big woman bit her bottom lip as if she were very worried now.

Patiently, the General waited for the prisoner to answer the first part of his question and when she didn't, he pressed on with, "Why did you kill him? Had Captain Colbert something to do with it?" Leclerc already knew the answer, or thought he did. In the confusion of the arrest, the gendarmes had swiftly searched Colbert's handbag and found the dildo. Obviously the dead man had attempted to induce the prisoner to have sex with the big woman.

"The fat perverted swine wanted me to perform for him with her!" she blurted out suddenly with a trace of her old spirit. "Something snapped and I killed him. I wish I could regret it, but I don't. He was worthless. He had betrayed everybody he had ever come into contact with, all his life."

Leclerc flashed an angry look at the big woman. "And he would have betrayed you, too, once he no longer needed you. That's how he and his kind went through life. He deserved to die." Solange started to cry, her skinny shoulders heaving like those of a heartbroken child.

Leclerc nodded to an aide and mouthed "Cognac."

The aide hastened outside and returned a moment later with a glass of brandy. Leclerc patted the girl on the shoulder and handed her the glass. "Take a sip of that," he said gently. "It will make you feel better, my dear. Look," he added, "I know you have done something very terrible, though I must say that it wasn't altogether unjustified." He waited until the girl took her first hesitant sip of the alcohol before adding, "But tell me what I want to know and then I promise you I will try to do my best for you."

The brandy had its warming, calming effect. She ceased crying and, looking up at him with her tear-stained, thin child's face, she said in a small voice, "The Party wanted to know when you planned to set off for your attack on Strasbourg. That's what I was ordered to find out from Joubert."

Leclerc whistled softly and looked around significantly at the grim faces of his staff officers. He knew they were thinking the same as he: the Communists were on to de Gaulle's plan for national unity already. That was bad.

"And what did you find out?" he continued in the same gentle manner as before. In truth he felt sorry for the girl. Before the war no court in France would have convicted the girl of murder. They would have put it down to a crime of passion. But not now, de Gaulle was ruthless with Communists whenever they transgressed the law. He would ensure that the girl was sentenced to death. It would be Madame Guillotine for her.

She shrugged as if she could read his mind and knew now that nothing was of importance any more.

"He told me that you had sent a group of English soldiers to find a route through the mountains for your division."

"And?"

"I can only guess, *mon general*, but I expect our people will attempt to destroy these Englishmen to delay your advance until the heavy snows come . . ." Leclerc glanced out of the window at the falling snow and she left the rest of her sentence uncompleted.

He knew what she meant though. Delay the advance another few days perhaps even hours and he would never get on the side roads that the *rostbifs* had found for him. The weather forecast was very bad indeed, he had already learned that this morning. He thought for a moment, then said as gently as before, "All right, my girl, I will ask no further questions." He held out his hand and his staff officers gasped. But the girl took it and he pressed her cold fingers a little and said, "Remember, I will try to do what I can for you."

"Thank you, *mon general*," she whispered sadly, knowing that Leclerc could do nothing for her.

He nodded to the two gendarmes. They advanced and took the girl by her skinny arms to lead her out. Leclerc waited till she had gone, then he turned to his senior aide and, iron in his voice, barked: "Arrest *Captaine* Colbert. She is to be placed under close arrest until the day of her court martial." He looked sternly at the suddenly ashen, big woman. "You are a disgrace to your uniform, to France and your sex. I cannot stand the sight of you any longer. Take her away!"

Colbert opened her mouth, as if to protest, but thought better of it. Tamely she let herself be escorted out by the senior aide.

Once she had gone, Leclerc sprang into action. "To the map, gentlemen," he ordered.

Hastily, his officers grouped themselves around the big tactical map of the Vosges with the Rhine plain beyond. An aide handed Leclerc a pointer. He tapped the forward slopes of the Vosges and barked, "So far the English have discovered no further German troops once they passed through the German line opposite the US 79th Division. So that means the actual boche line is a thin shell, easily cracked."

There was murmur of agreement from the assembled officers.

"Now to the best of out knowledge the first sizeable German garrisons which we will encounter," Leclerc continued, "are – there – guarding the Saverne Gap at Phalsbourg – here – and Saverne itself. If either of those garrison towns is alerted in advance of our attack, we are doomed to failure. The Germans could hold us off for days and in that time they could easily reinforce Strasbourg from across the Rhine. So surprise has to be everything. We must seize both towns by a *coup de main*. Is that understood?"

"*L'audace, toujours l'audace et encore l'audace*," a deep bass voice boomed, quoting that famous motto: "For a boche, that Prussian Frederick the Great knew of what he spoke."

Leclerc smiled. It was Colonel Dio, his old comrade of Kufra, who was one of the few surviving who had been with him right from the start. "*Hein mon vieux Dio*," he said. "*On y est, cette fois.* You shall lead!"

Dio's face lit up. "Strasbourg is mine!" he exclaimed.

"*Exactement!*" Leclerc answered.

"When do I start *mon general?*" Dio asked excitedly.

105

Leclerc looked at the snowflakes whirling back and forth outside the window. "Weather forecasts suggest that the current snowfall will end just before dawn, my dear Dio. You will start then. Your main axis of advance will be along the route the English have mapped out for us."

"But we don't want your column to be too long. That could lead to delays. Take any tracks and ways you can find to left and right of that route. Five or six if necessary."

Dio opened his mouth to protest, but Leclerc beat him to it. "I know, Dio, I know," he said. "That appears to dissipate our efforts, but we can soon regroup on the main route if we meet the boche, which I doubt we will."

Dio put on his kepi hastily. He swept Leclerc a magnificent salute, the kind they had given each other as boy cadets back in St Cyr the French military academy, when they had been young, innocent and happy. "There is much to be done, *mon general*," he announced. "You will see me again at Saverne."

Leclerc nodded. He couldn't return the salute because he did not have his own kepi. "France depends upon you, Dio," he said grandly.

"Trust me, General, I will not let France down. I —"

The rest of his words were drowned by a sudden shrill scream, followed an instant later by a burst of machine-pistol fire and angry shouts.

"God in heaven! *What is that?*" Leclerc shouted.

A few moments later he found out. A gendarme, his dark-blue uniform covered in snow, burst into the map room breathlessly. "It's the girl, General," he panted, chest heaving with the effort. "She's —"

Leclerc brushed past him, followed by his staff, into the howling storm. Flashlights were trying to penetrate the white gloom. Men shouted, their voice muffled by the snow. Somewhere, the bells of an ambulance tingled. "Over here, sir!" a gendarme cried, flashing his torch at the staff officers.

Leclerc hurried, eyes blinking in the snow. A gendarme loomed up out of the storm. He saluted. "There she is, sir," he said and flashed his torch on the ground. "We couldn't stop her. We didn't think —"

Leclerc held up his hand for silence. The gendarme stopped speaking immediately. The General stared down at the dead girl, crumpled, body twisted and awkward, outlined by a star of her own blood on the surface of the snow.

"She jumped," someone said.

Slowly, very slowly, Leclerc raised his hand to his forehead in a last salute. "She died," he said tonelessly, as if speaking to himself. "She died bravely. In her way, she, too, died for France." Then he turned and headed for the shaft of yellow light coming from the open door, his head bowed.

Chapter Six

It was 'Tashy' Kennedy who first heard them. Tired as he had been after the long day's reconnaissance in the biting cold of the mountain, "the old urge" as he called it, had still been there. All the while the plump little maid had served them their stew, he had watched her every movement and an amused Stevens had muttered, "You fancy her, don't yer, Tashy!"

"Something rotten, Stevie," he had answered his running mate. "If I got up now I'd knock the frigging mugs off the table if yer get what I mean?"

His comrade had.

"I'd like to get the drawers off'n her, woollen or not," he had remarked and had succeeded with decided ease, though he only spoke a few words of French and no German, the maid's native language. But as he had always boasted to anyone prepared to listen, "The language of love is in yer trousers, mate. That's all that Tashy needs to get 'em on their backs with the pearly gates spread wide."

Not that Tashy had needed to speak much. When the others were asleep, save for the sentry in the main house, he had crept in stockinged feet to her little chamber above the pig-sty, where she slept on a straw mattress warmed by the heat coming from the snoring pigs below. Barely had she woken, than

108

she was eagerly pulling off her cotton night dress to reveal her plump, nubile body in the light of the candle she had lit hastily. "Right randy, she were," he would tell Stevens later. "At it like a fiddler's elbow, muttering away all the time as if she couldn't get enough of it."

He had taken her a couple of times and then they had happily dozed off in each others' arms. That was until Tashy had first heard the rusty squeak of tracks and as he sat up, wide awake instantly, he knew that the only tracked vehicles in these mountains would be German!

Hastily, he tiptoed to the tiny dirty window and rubbed it clear. The girl naked as she was, followed him and peered over his shoulder. He squinted into the gloom, trying to catch some kind of outline against the white background of the snow. But it was the girl who spotted the intruders first. "*Da . . . d-druben,*" she hissed and when saw he didn't understand, added in French, "*Lá – lá bas!*"

Tashy followed the direction of her finger. He nodded grimly. She was right. There were two dark shapes just beyond the trees to the right of the house and on the road he could see the outline of what looked like a half track.

"*Schlechte Leute,*" she whispered fearfully. "*Mechant Gestapo.*"

Tashy understood that last word all right. They had been on the run from the German secret police for months now. Hurriedly he grabbed his trousers, tagged them on, pulled his boots from the pockets and put them on too. He gave the little naked girl a hasty kiss, slapped her plump rump and said, "Back into

109

kipp, toot sweet." With a nod of his head, he indicated the straw mattress.

She understood. Hastily she slipped under the rough covers and pulled the blanket right over her head.

Swiftly, Tashy moved down the long hall that smelled of apples and hard work. "Stevie!" he whispered to the shadowy figure sitting in a hard-back chair near the main door, Sten gun across his knees, obviously waiting for his hour of 'stag' to end. "There's somebody out there. I'm going to alert the boss."

Stevens was wide awake immediately. He clicked the safety catch off on his Sten and tapped the magazine to see if it was fitted correctly. "With yer, Tashy" he whispered. He rose and crept to the fogged-up window while Tashy went to where Paddy Mayne lay next to O'Sullivan in the line of snoring men huddled in their grey Army blankets.

Hurriedly Tashy bent down close to the snoring giant, pressed his lips to his right ear and at the same time placed his hand over Paddy Mayne's mouth. "Boss!" he whispered urgently.

Mayne sat up at once, then realising whose hand was holding his mouth, he nodded to indicate he knew there was some danger so that Tashy was able to release his hold on Paddy's mouth. "What is it?"

"Trouble outside. Think they're Jerries, Boss."

Without another word, Paddy slipped into his boots, and pulled out his Colt. "Where?"

Five minutes later the whole room was alerted, putting on their equipment in the dark, reaching for their weapons. By then Rory and Stevens had already assessed their position. There was one or more half tracks on the mountain road some 50 yards away and it was clear that there were armed men in the trees all around the farmhouse. There had also been a muffled howl that might have been a wild animal, but Rory, crouched in the freezing cold just outside the door, said to Tashy, "Could be tracker dogs. The Hun often uses them."

Back in the big room with the troopers assembled, ready for action, Paddy Mayne said urgently, "All right, we're not to stay and fight. We're going to do a bunk."

"They'll hear the Jeeps starting up, Boss," someone objected.

"They won't if we don't start them up," Mayne answered. "I think they'll expect us to continue up the mountain road. We won't. We roll down the road we came with the engines off. Once we're clear, then we'll start up and double back. Clear?"

There was murmur of assent from his men.

"If there's anyone on the track leading to the road, nobble 'em with your coshes. Anyone makes a noise," he clenched a fist like a small steam shovel, "I'll have his guts for garters." He let the words sink in. "I'll take the lead. Rory and Smithie there will bring up the rear."

"Yes, Boss," Rory said hastily. "I —" He stopped suddenly. A door had creaked behind them. It was the one-handed farmer in his undershirt and long, baggy underpants. He had a candle-stick holder in his hand. His intention was obvious, he was going to light it in a moment. That light would certainly alert the intruders. Instinctively Rory felt that the farmer had been the one who had betrayed them to the enemy somehow or other.

He reacted instinctively. His fist flashed and the blow caught the farmer on the jaw who gave a little gasp and began to sink to the bare flags, the candle-stick holder still clutched in his good hand. Rory caught them both just in time. He lowered the unconscious farmer the rest of the way noiselessly. Paddy Mayne nodded his approval. "Come on," he hissed. "Let's get the hell out of here while there's still time."

They needed no urging. They knew that once the cannon which the half-tracks carried started opening fire the farmhouse could be a death-trap. Hastily but noiselessly they filed outside into the bitting cold. They stole across the yard, grateful for the muffling snow now, to where the Jeeps were parked.

Mayne gave no orders. He didn't need to. His men had been through this sort of thing often enough. Each man knew his job exactly. While the driver released the brake, the other three men of the Jeep team took the strain and started to push the little vehicle across the farmyard towards the track leading to the road.

Up front, while the signaller, Stevens, steered the Jeep, Mayne pushed mightily, as if he were back in some match-winning rugby scrum before the war. Slowly, but surely the three of them started to edge the Jeep towards the track, each man praying that they wouldn't be spotted out in the open. Behind them, the others did the same: they were a little fleet of squat vehicles, outlined in stark black against the whiteness of the snowfield.

All was silent. There was no sound from the enemy.

112

The only noise was the soft crunch of the Jeeps' tyres on the snow. Mayne's vehicle reached the track. The farmer had cleared the snow so now the going was easier. The Jeep started to roll forward more quickly. Mayne began to feel happier, so far the enemy hadn't tumbled to their escape attempt. Another 20 yards and they'd be on the road and rolling downhill. They were going to do it!

"Boss," Stevens hissed suddenly.

"What is it?" Mayne hissed back.

"To the front at eleven o'clock."

Mayne looked up sharply and peered into the gloom to the left, further up the track. A dark shape had detached itself from the shadows cast by some skeletal bushes. Christ! He cursed to himself. It was a vicious Dobermann pinscher, one of the hunting dogs, German police used. "Keep her rolling," he whispered, "I'll deal with the bugger."

Crouched low, presenting the smallest silhouette possible for a man of his size, he crept forward, making little sound. But the hound must have scented him. It raised its vicious snout and sniffed the keen air. Still he kept on going. Behind him, the troopers continued pushing their Jeeps up the track towards the road.

A low growl came from deep down within the Dobermann. Paddy Mayne swallowed hard. In a moment he'd have to make his move.

The dog bared its yellow teeth and growled again, low and menacing. Slowly, very slowly, it went back on its haunches, ears pricked, tail low between its legs.

Paddy braced himself as the dog launched itself forward, as it had been trained to do. A hundred pounds of muscle and flesh struck the big Ulsterman. But the man, who had won half a dozen caps for rugby and toured South Africa with the British Lions team, took the shock as he always had on the rugby field. He staggered, but didn't go down. Viciously the hound raked his face with its claws. Paddy bit back a cry of pain and clamped his big hand, with which he was could tear telephone books apart, around the beast's muzzle.

Desperately the animal struggle to get free as its air supply was cut off, squirming wildly back and forth. Again its claws ripped across Paddy's face but he held on. Suddenly, the dog threw itself to one side. Paddy Mayne was not taken in by the trick. He rolled down with the dog. Now the hound's breath was giving out, its struggles were becoming weaker. Paddy Mayne knew he had almost won, but he couldn't waste any more time on the beast. With all the strength of his 6 ft 5 in frame, he jerked the Dobermann's jaw up and to one side. There was an ugly click, the hound's spine arched crazily. Next moment it was dead.

For a moment, Paddy Mayne just lay with it in the snow, holding its muzzle in his grip of steel and panting heavily. Then, as the first Jeep started to roll by him noiselessly, he knew he had to get up. He scrambled to his feet, wiping away the blood dripping from his scratched face, and applied his massive strength to the right rear wheel. The Jeep slammed on to the road. Still the enemy had not reacted.

Now more and more Jeeps started to assemble on the mountain road, bonnets facing downwards, while the teams formed up in defensive perimeters, ready for

114

action. Mayne wasn't going to start until they were all assembled. Then he hoped they would free-wheel downwards noiselessly and together and start up their engines once they were round the second bend. He reasoned that the German half-tracks wouldn't be able to catch up with the faster Jeeps, especially as the latter would have had a head start.

Up ahead in the gloomy firs there was a low whistle and someone called softly, "*Lux, wo bist du, Junge?*" It was a handler calling for his dog, Mayne guessed that right away. There was no time to be lost. The handler would probably come looking for the ugly beast in a minute. "Mount up," he breathed.

Quick as lightning, the men sprang into their Jeeps. The drivers released their brakes while the men at the rear gave a kick on the road. The vehicles started to roll. Now they were on the descent. Suddenly they were going all out, the drivers leaning intently over their steering-wheels and peering into the darkness, for they were driving without lights. Behind there was a sudden shout, followed a moment later by a burst of white tracer. A motor started up and then another. They had been discovered. The chase was on . . .

Chapter Seven

"Sod this for a game of soldiers!" Sergeant Smith grunted angrily. Once again he had let out the clutch and again nothing had happened. The engine hadn't started.

"Give it another ten seconds," Rory said urgently, as they whizzed round another corner in the mountain road, with the other Jeeps now a long way ahead of them. "It should start then."

"I think the motor's duff mesen," Smith said through gritted teeth, as he concentrated on the road, still in darkness for their lights, too, had refused to come on.

Behind them the rattle of tracks was getting louder. It was clear that the German half-tracks were gaining on them. Rory O'Sullivan started to make contingency plans, just in case.

Seeming to read his thoughts, Tashy at the seat and balancing the best he could, stood up and swung the twin Browning machine-guns on their tripod round to face the rear.

They swung round another bend, narrowly grazing the snow-heavy bank.

"Watch it, Sarge," Tashy shouted. "You nearly lost me then!"

Hunched over the wheel, not taking his eyes off the

road ahead for a second, Smith shouted back, "You'd make a lovely corpse, with that frigging moustache of yours!"

At any other time, Rory would have laughed. The men seemed to be able to keep up their spirits even in the direst of situations. But not now. He knew that they wouldn't survive if they were taken alive. Through his mind there flashed a picture of those two poor mutilated SAS troopers taken by the unknown Dr Barsch and his torturers. The same thing would happen to them if they didn't succeed in getting away now. "Try it again, Smithie," he yelled above the roar of the wind as they surged down to the flat ground where they would roll to a stop if they couldn't start the Jeep's motor.

"OK, Boss," Smithie yelled back. He rattled off a silent prayer, depressed the clutch and then, counting to three let it out again. *Nothing*! The engine made no response whatsoever. "Frig it," he said.

"No go?" Rory cried.

"No go, Boss."

"Right!" Rory made a snap decision. "We stop behind the next bend. Tashy, get ready with that Chicago piano." He meant the twin Browning .5 machine-guns.

"What yer gonna do, Boss?" Smith asked urgently.

"Stop that half-track, if we can. Then we'll radio the C.O. to come back and give us a tow, if he can."

"It's gonna be nip-and-tuck," Smith yelled, as behind them the clatter of the tracked vehicle grew ever louder. The Germans were definitely gaining on them.

"That's what makes life exciting, Smithie!" Rory

117

cried and fumbled for the bag of grenades behind his seat.

They swung round the bend. "Hit the anchors, Smithie," he ordered.

Even as he did, slowing down very reluctantly, Rory was out of the Jeep and charging up the embankment to the left, while Tashy readied himself behind the machine-guns.

Panting with the effort, Rory pelted up the incline, up to his knees in snow. He swung himself over the top and stumbled to the bend.

The half-track, followed by another vehicle he couldn't quite make out, was rattling down the mountain road, its rear packed with helmeted soldiers. Rory grinned wickedly. They were going to be easy meat, he told himself. He took a grenade from the bag suspended from his shoulder and pulled out the pin. Down below Tashy tensed behind the 'Chicago piano'.

Now the half-track was almost to the bend, its brakes squeaking shrilly as the driver prepared to take the curve. It was slowing down nicely, thought Rory as he prepared to launch the first grenade into space, eyes fixed on the open rear of the enemy vehicle. "*One, two, three*," counting off the seconds. He let go of the pin and it flew away. Now the grenade was armed. "*Four!*" he cried aloud and threw it, grabbing into the bag for a second one the next instant.

The grenade fell right into the well of the open rear of the half-track. It exploded in an angry flash of violet flame. The rear end of the half track shuddered. Frantically, the driver hit the brakes, his back ripped to shreds, as the engine burst into flames.

The doomed vehicle, already filled with its cargo of dead and dying soldiers, skidded around the corner straight into the concentrated fire from Tashy's twin machine-guns. It was heading into a solid wall of white tracer. The dying driver screamed one more time and fell dead over the shattered wheel. Next moment the half-track careened off the road, scattering bodies as it did so and began to buck and bolt its way down the steep slope to the right of the mountain road, to explode below in a massive burst of flame.

Behind it, the second vehicle – Rory could make out it was a French truck, a Renault, he guessed – skidded to a halt. Figures in dark blue flung themselves out of it and, crouching low, began to fire. "*Milice!*" Rory yelled and flung another grenade at them, knowing they were far out of range. Uselessly, the grenade exploded in the middle of the road. All the same, it did the trick. The *Milice* began to pull back, firing still, but definitely withdrawing as if they suspected there was a superior force hidden round the bend.

Rory waited no longer. He skidded and slithered down the bend. "Get her rolling again," he gasped to Smith. "We've stopped the buggers for a while. Anyway, they'll take their time for a while."

Smith released the brake. Rory gave a push and swung himself on. Slowly they started to roll towards the flat. They had done it again . . .

Chretien slapped his swagger stick down on the desk angrily and barked into the mouthpiece of the telephone, "Someone will answer to me for this! You had a perfect set-up and you let the *rostbifs* get away like that! A lot of bungling amateurs." He lost patience with his informant and slammed the phone down so violently that the bell jingled.

"Well?" Barsch demanded eagerly.

Chretien gave him a black and angry look. "They let the damn English get away – and 20 young SS grenadiers are dead to no purpose. *Mensch, das ist zum Kotzen.*"*

Barsch sucked on a hollow tooth at the back of his mouth and thought, while Chretien glowered through the window of his office at the street below. German officers with their wives and mistresses sauntered along the pavement, smartly returning the salutes of private soldiers as if this was some damned peacetime garrison, he told himself angrily, not a city that might well be caught up in a fierce battle within a matter of days.

"Ambush," Barsch broke the heavy brooding silence.

Chretien looked at him, as if he had suddenly gone out of his mind. "What do you mean, *ambush?*" he demanded savagely.

"I'm not much of a military man," Barsch answered with unusual modesty for him. "But by looking at the map, one can predict where these English swine are going to come out of the mountains."

Chretien's face lit up for the first time since he had heard that the attempt to take the *rostbifs* at the farm had failed. "Of course, of course!" he agreed enthusiastically. He strode over to the big map of Alsace behind his desk, while Barsch, obviously pleased with himself, took out that dreadful tobacco

* Literally, "Man, it's sick-making."

120

pouch – "My Jewish tit," as he always described it to anyone who enquired, and stuffed some of the mixture into his pipe.

"Here – at the Saverne Gap," Chretien said after a few moments' perusal of the map. "You Prussians used it back in 1870 and then the *Wehrmacht* did again in 1940. The Saverne Gap is the only exit from the Northern Vosges. Leclerc will have to come through it if he's heading for Strasbourg."

Barsch, puffing at his pipe now, walked over to the map and stared at it with Chretien. Outside, the band was playing merrily, all brass and drums, as the guards marched to the daily parade at what was now called *Adolf Hitler Platz*.

Chretien frowned. "Great crap on the Christmas Tree!" he exclaimed. "There they go again, playing soldiers again as if this was 1940 and *not* 1944, when the tick-tock really is in the pisspot!"

Barsch didn't react to the outburst. It was no concern of his. His sole purpose was to save his own skin. If they didn't stop the English this time, he would have to put the pressure on that fat fool of a Professor to get permission from Himmler to take his damn stupid collection of bits and pieces of human bodies across the Rhine. "There are quite a few roads leading into the Gap. Will we have enough troops and *Milice* to cover them all, Commandant?"

"I don't think we will be needing any troops at all," Chretien answered calmly, the plan unfurling in his mind perfectly, as if it had been there all the time.

"What do you mean?" Barsch asked, puzzled.

Chretien turned from the map and looked at Barsch directly with that evil, scarred face of his. "We can let

121

other people pick the chestnuts out of the fire for us," he answered.

"Other people?"

"Yes, the Reds."

"*The Reds?*"

"Yes," Chretien answered thoughtfully. "Hagenau and Saverne have plenty of Reds in the factories there. They are not Alsatians, they come mainly from Lorraine round Metz way and Metz has always been a hot bed of Communism."

He warmed to his theme. "Most of them are armed already and the Russians are shipping in more guns via Marseilles by the day. If we and you Germans looked the other way they could set up roadblocks on all those entry roads to the Gap."

Barsch whistled softly. "What a devious race you French —"

"*Alsatian* in my case," Chretien interrupted him sternly tapping his chest. "We're a different breed altogether."

"All right, *the* French," Barsch conceded, puffing at his pipe. "Using one group to do your dirty work against the third party, for you. Such deviousness is too much for the simple German mind."

Chretien didn't comment on the "simple German mind". These days, with his world falling apart, he had no time for "classy chats about the cosmos." Instead, he said, "At the same time, Barsch, I think you should alert the German garrisons at Hagenau, Saverne and Phalsbourg about what might be coming their way."

"I don't know about that —" Barsch began as the phone on Chretien's desk started to ring urgently. The latter snatched the phone and snapped, "*Commandant*

Chretien, ich hore —" He listened eagerly and then changed over to French, "*Quand?*" he demanded.

Again he listened eagerly and said, "*Une quinzaine de pieces avec leurs trains?*"

At the other end, the person he was speaking to must have agreed, and Chretien snapped, "*Le deuxieme element?*"

Again he listened and then with a brisk "*merci,*" he put the phone down and turned to Barsch, who was waiting anxiously; he guessed from the look on the Alsatian's face that something important had happened. Chretien didn't beat about the bush. He said, "Leclerc has moved. Two of his amoured columns have slipped through the German front in the High Vosges and are on their way."

"*Scheisse!*" Barsch cursed and told himself he was wasting time by playing along with Chretien and his crazy schemes. Germany was no longer going to win the war whatever happened here in France. If the Anglo-Americans couldn't beat the Reich, the Russians to the East would. Why else would Stalin and his Russians be actively sabotaging the Western Allies by supplying France's Communists if they didn't think they could beat Germany single-handed? Of course, the Russian dictator, with his armies poised on Germany's eastern frontiers, was confident that he could go it alone. Perhaps he even thought he was powerful enough to roll right through the Reich and into Western Europe.

Chretien must have noticed the look on Barsch's face for he snapped, "Something wrong?"

"No, no," Barsch lied speedily. "Just thinking, that's all."

123

"Well, don't do so. The time has come for action, not thoughts," Chretien barked.

Barsch nodded, as if in agreement. To himself he said, "But not with you old horse. Emil Barsch has now decided he has made a separate peace. For him the war is over . . ."

Chapter Eight

"*We must have faith,*" the Führer cried in that hoarse Austrian voice of his, which still sent shivers down Chretien's spine whenever he heard it. "*Faith to conquer . . . faith to win . . . faith to take on the whole world if necessary . . . and if we finally fail . . . then we shall drag down half the universe with us . . . in fire and ashes . . . !*"

The wild, excited cries of "*Sieg Heil*" and "*Heil mein Fuhrer!*" were drowned by the brassy blare of military bands and the harsh martial stamp of thousands of jackboots, as the soldiers of the Reich, each one undoubtedly a blond giant, goose-stepped past their beloved Führer.

Chretien breathed out hard. Suddenly, as the record ended, he felt drained of emotion. Why had he to live in these days of decline, he asked himself, when the only way to survive was to be a cynic?

He turned the record, wound the gramophone up once more and settled down with his cheroot to wait for the informer. Wagner's noble music of the *Gotterdammerung* flooded the room, which he maintained for these meetings in the working-class quarter of Strasbourg, near the main railway station.

Chretien indulged himself a little as he waited, thinking of the past and what might have been if the

Germans had not been such fools. Back in 1940, they had had the working-class French eating out of their hands. They had given them full employment working in the war factories or in the Reich itself. The peasants were happy, too. They had been getting better prices for their produce than ever before. And naturally the great industrialists were happy. Not only were their factories working at full capacity, they were also no longer troubled by strikes or industrial unrest which had been such a thorn in their flesh during the Third Republic.

But when there had been trouble here and there, the Gestapo and SS had stepped in. Their methods knew no subtlety. He remembered how horrified he had been at their methods back in 1942, cigarettes stubbed on prisoners' faces, urinating in the mouths of suspects, the 'water treatment', prisoners held under water until they thought they were drowning . . .

As the Wagner came to an end unnoticed, Chretien, moodily puffing at his cheroot, thought of that occasion when that gigantic Gestapo thug *Oberkommissar* Dahl had had a waif of a girl suspect stripped naked in front of his jeering colleagues, had had her whipped and when she still wouldn't confess, he had lost his temper. Grabbing the terrified victim by the ankles and exerting all his brutal strength he had whirled her round and round to the shoots and applause of the onlookers. Then tiring of the sport, he had flung the screaming terrified child away from him to slam into the opposite wall. Her head had split open like an over-ripe melon and her brains had splashed out in a great grey-red flurry of revolting matter.

Brutality had bred brutality. Opposition to the

126

Germans and their French Vichy allies had grown and grown. Both sides had fought savagely, showing no mercy. Quarter was neither given nor expected. Inevitably he, too, had become used to the sadistic cruelty of his German comrades-in-arms.

He had not noticed it at first, but slowly he had come to realise that he, too, was obsessed by the heady excitement of torture and sadism, the slow but brutal breaking of a prisoner's physical and mental personality. Indeed it had become more important to him than wealth, women or promotion.

He knew there was no chance of turning the clock back. But still the rot might be stopped before it was too late and disaster struck? One had to try.

There was a soft, furtive knock on the door of the shabby room. It was his informant Jo-Jo.

Hastily, Chretien rose to his feet, clearing his mind immediately of his doubts. As an afterthought, just before he opened the door, he concealed his second pistol beneath the '*Volkischer Beobachter*', newspaper which lay on little round table in front of him.

Then he placed his service pistol in the pocket of his civilian jacket, for he had changed from his *Milice* uniform in order not to compromise his informant in case the latter was being followed. "*Ich komme,*" he called as Jo-Jo tapped again, and hurried to the door.

Hardly had he opened it when Jo-Jo, a little runt of a man with a loose sensual mouth, had slipped in, closing the door with a back kick of his foot. "Can't be too careful," he breathed, dark eyes searching the shabby room for danger, as if he saw assassins everywhere. "They'd slit my gizzard just like that," he clicked his dirty thumb and forefinger together, "if they knew I was working for you, Commandant." He sat without being asked and reached for one of Chretien's cheroots.

"You're not working for me Jo-Jo," Chretien commented cynically, "you're working for yourself." He indicated the twin heaps of silver coins on the table beyond the German newspaper. "There's your wages, if you come through with this one."

Jo-Jo licked his red lips greedily, eyeing the coins. "What have I got to do?" he asked in the accented German of Lorraine, the province he came from. "You know my comrades —"

"They're not your frigging comrades," Chretien interrupted sharply, eyeing the runtish, unshaven face and telling himself that he couldn't allow people like Jo-Jo to run France. Even de Gaulle's lot were better than the Reds. He knew that if he wanted to get the crook to do as he wanted he had to put Jo-Jo in his place. With those eyes of his, about which colleagues said could strip a man naked mentally in 30 seconds flat, fixed on the other man, he said severely, "Listen, let's get this straight. You are a cheap little crooked pervert, Jo-Jo. You started off stealing women's knickers off clothes lines in Metz, where you were born, as a kid."

"It was all a mistake — " Jo-Jo began, but Chretien silenced him with a rough, "*Halt die Schnauze* – hold your trap, you scum!"

Jo-Jo held his "trap".

"Then at 14 you were nicked flashing yer sugar stick at kids outside a girls' school."

Jo-Jo looked glumly at the table, but didn't interrupt.

128

"When you did your national service before the war in the Maginot Line you were caught doing something unpleasant to a cow." He laughed coarsely at Jo-Jo, whose sly face was slowly turning red. "You must have a nice big sugar stick to do that, ha ha! If you hadn't *volunteered* to join the Foreign Legion at Sidi-Bel-Abbes, they would have sent you to Devil's Island for that." He let his words sink in before adding, "No, you don't fool me, Jo-Jo. But no matter, if you pull this off for me, there is more than that heap of coins for you."

Jo-Jo's embarrassment vanished. "What is in it for me?"

"A new pass which means a new life and enough money to keep you in the South of France for a year. They'll never find you there – *your comrades,*" he emphasised the words contemptuously.

"What do you want me to do?" Jo-Jo asked hesitantly.

Chretien told him.

When he was finished Jo-Jo looked at him aghast. "Block every road out of the moutains into the Saverne Gap!" he stuttered. "How would I get that sort of information, that the *rostbifs* were leading Leclerc's Gaullist Fascists?"

Chretien told himself that Jo-Jo, petty crook and pervert had quickly adopted the Reds' double talk – "Gaullist fascists" indeed! Aloud, he said, "You have a friend in the *Milice*, my Strasbourg *Milice*," he said firmly, as if he had total confidence in his proposal.

"He's like you. He likes putting on women's knickers. You've got something in common, as it were. He's passed the information on to you for the price of a soiled pair of black frilly knickers stolen from a high-born lady here in Strasbourg. How does that sound to you as a cover story? No one could invent anything more bizarre than that, eh, Jo-Jo?" He looked winningly at the evil little man.

Once this operation was over, he told himself grimly, Jo-Jo and all his other informants would disappear suddenly without trace. He had done it before and he could do again, he had to consider his own future if anything went wrong. He wanted no one left alive who might point the finger at him. Perhaps Barsch would have to go, he considered thoughtfully, while he waited for the traitor's decision.

Jo-Jo licked his lips, looked at the pile of coins and then back at Chretien's hard, unrevealing face. "If I did decide to do it, how would I put it across to the committee – I mean the collection of comrades, who make the decision?"

"Listen, Jo-Jo, they probably know as much about you as I do. They know what kind of pervert you are. So you put it on the line: how your fellow knicker pervert —"

Jo-Jo flushed red, again, but said nothing.

"Told you about the *rostbifs*, you now look embarrassed, but at the same time determined as if everything is for the cause, that's why you are revealing your terrible secret." Chretien laughed harshly. "The fact that you've got your information that way – from a *Milicien*, too, will go in your favour. They'll believe you all right."

"*Bon*," Jo-Jo said. "*Mais les allemands —*"

"Don't speak that decadent language to me, Jo-Jo,"

130

Chretien interrupted him harshly, "*Hier spricht man deutsch.*"

"All right, all right," Jo-Jo said impatiently. "But *why*, if the *Milice* know the *rostbifs* are coming, don't the Germans try to set up road-blocks on the road leading out of the Saverne Gap and *why* will they allow us to do it? That's the sort of thing the committee will ask."

Chretien was ready with an answer. "Because, one – the Germans don't have the troops to spare for routine duties like roadblocks." His eyes narrowed to evil slits. "And, two – they think your *comrades*," he emphasised the word again contemptuously, "are the *Milice*, assisting them in such routine work."

Jo-Jo puffed out his skinny, unshaved cheeks and whistled softly. "*Oh, la, la,*" he chortled. "That's right! Communists posing, as *Miliciens*. But they'll buy it."

"They certainly will," Chretien agreed eagerly, knowing that he had won the little pervert over, "especially as your knicker-sniffing, wearing friend of the *Milice* will provide our ID cards for every comrade in charge of a road-block. If any German gets too nosy, there will be a genuine *Milice* identity card, proving that the man in charge is a bonafide member of my organisation."

Jo-Jo nodded his head. "Yes that should do it. I think they'll buy that idea all right, Commandant."

"Of course they will," Chretien agreed with forced heartiness. "Well, Jo-Jo?"

"I'll do it, Commandant," the runt said enthusiastically. "I will indeed. But you will remember that pass and so on?"

131

"That I will, *Alter Freund*." He indicated the coins on the table. "Take them please."

Jo-Jo didn't need a second invitation. Moments later he was gone, slinking down the street, looking anxiously to left and right to see if anyone had spotted him, like the cunning little rat he was.

For a few minutes, Commandant Chretien watched him go, satisfied that he wasn't being followed or observed. Then he lit another cheroot and thought for a while in the shabby grey room, the only sound the rusty squeak of the bed-springs above where the 50-franc whore blousy and balloon-breasted, had her working-man clients. His mood had improved.

In 24 hours the *rostbifs* would be dead and Leclerc's drive would be stymied. He stared out of the dirty window at the leaden sky, which indicated more snow soon. Yes, perhaps there was yet a chance?

Outside, the boy in the ragged coat with wooden shoes on his feet, stopped collecting the *kippen*, fag-ends, from the frozen gutters. He looked to left and right to see if he had been observed. He hadn't. He started to follow Commandant Chretien.

Chapter Nine

It was a strange night of driving snow, full of sudden alarms and panics. The mountain roads were terrifyingly slick with huge drops to one side and it took all the drivers' skill to negotiate them. Time and time again a Jeep would skid and threaten to go over the side, then be brought to rest at the very last moment. As Sergeant Smith breathed to Rory O'Sullivan after yet another near disaster, "When I look tomorrow morning, you can bet your bottom dollar, boss, that my cellular drawers are a bright yeller." To which Rory, a little shaky himself, replied, "You can say that again, Smithie."

But it wasn't only the terrible weather that worried the little group of SAS troopers crossing those snow-bound mountains that night. There were men out there as well. They knew that for certain, but whether they were German or French Maquis they didn't know and they didn't attempt to find out. Once, they heard the sounds of shouting some way off. On another occasion, a flare hushed into the snow-filled sky to their right and hung there, burning a bright, incandescent white for what seemed an eternity. On a second occasion, there was a burst of red and green tracer to their immediate front. Paddy Mayne ordered the column to halt

133

and together with Stevens, his radio operator, he went forward on foot through the driving snow to investigate. But when he returned, looking like a snow giant with snowflakes plastered all over his massive frame, he reported, "Nothing. Not a bloody sausage!"

About 3 a.m. the road started to descend and Rory, bringing up the rear with Smith, reasoned they were slowly beginning to come down from the High Vosges. An hour later they began to pass through half-finished positions, trenches already filled with snow, and barbed wire entanglements. They were German all right, it was obvious. They had covered their dugouts with freshly-cut logs and only Germans went to that kind of trouble with positions they might well have to abandon a day later.

Now, Paddy Mayne decided they should have a rest before they came out of the mountains altogether. "Into those two shacks," he ordered, shouting against the howl of the snowstorm. "Get the tommy cookers," meaning the little petrol stoves that the SAS used, "and brew up. You've got half an hour to sort yourselves out."

The frozen, weary troopers needed no urging. Within five minutes they had pumped up the pressure in the little cookers and were boiling mess tins full of melted snow to make the 'char' that they all craved, while others broke open the compo ration boxes and did the same with tins of 'M & V' – meat and vegetable stew.

Fifteen minutes later, their pinched, frozen face wreathed in steam, they were wolfing down stew and hard biscuits, followed by tremendous gulps of burningly hot 'Sarnt Major's char', a new light in their faded eyes.

"We'll remember rough-and-ready meals like this long after we've forgotten the best the Savoy or Connaught can dish up, Rory, me lad," Paddy Mayne said, spearing a piece of the cheap meat from the M & Vstew. He looked round at the men with their weatherbeaten, red faces, eating the same simple fare, and added, "those of us who survive will always think of these times."

Rory nodded and for an instant he caught a glint that might have been a tear in the big Ulsterman's eyes. "Well, well!" he said to himself with surprise. "Old Paddy's a sentimentalist at heart."

It was just then that Stevens, the handsome young blond wireless operator came across to the two officers. "Just heard from the French, Boss," he said without any preamble.

Paddy Mayne, strict disciplinarian that he was, had always frowned on "that Army bullshit. You know, if it moves, salute it. If it doesn't, paint it white."

Their leading elements are about twelve hours behind us," said Stevens.

Paddy nodded, "Thanks, Stevie. Go and get yourself some grub and char before yon Tashy scoffs it all up."

Stevens nodded. "Yes, Boss. Don't worry. I'll get me share."

Paddy Mayne put down his combined fork and spoon for a moment, while he did a quick calculation. "That means," he said, "Leclerc's point is about 12 to 20 miles behind us, depending on how fast they can move on these wretched roads."

135

"So, with luck they'll catch up with us late tomorrow night," Rory said.

"Yes, and by then we'll have done our recce of the Saverne Gap." He lifted up his mess tin and took another spoonful of the stew. "It'll be our task to ensure that the French don't get held up there. Once they're through they can reach Strasbourg in a day, with a bit of luck." Paddy Mayne unwittingly echoed General Leclerc. "Then it'll be speed and surprise that'll do the trick for his chaps."

Rory nodded his agreement and regretfully drained the last of his 'sarnt-major's char' from the clumsy, square mess tin. "Then we go after that murderous Dr Barsch, if he's still in Strasbourg."

"Don't worry, Rory, I haven't forgotten about him, the swine. Once we've got the French through the Gap, our contract, as we used to say in my old profession is at an end."

He grinned and Rory did the same. Rory O'Sullivan could hardly imagine him dressed as a pre-war solicitor in striped trousers and bowler, for that had once been this tough giant's profession.

"Then we're on our own and Winnie Churchill or whoever is behind this mission will have to do without us for a little while."

Ten minutes later, feeling a lot better, they were battling through the raging snowstorm once more, but gradually as they drove lower and lower, the snow changed first to sleet and then in the end to driving rain that came down in sheets.

Dawn came reluctantly, as if some God on high hesitated to illuminate the crazy, war-torn world below. But as the little convoy, well spread out

136

now, came rolling out of the foothills, coming ever closer to the Rhine plain below, the grey light of a November dawn started to flush the winter sky. Once they stopped and the two SAS officers surveyed their front.

On the horizon they could just make out plumes of smoke ascending to the sky and Paddy commented, "That must be Saverne. According to my map there must be at least seven minor and three major roads running into the place."

"I suppose what we want is one that doesn't run into Saverne but skirts it and heads off south-east towards Strasbourg."

"Exactly," the giant agreed. "But we'll take it easy and see what we can do. Remember, though, Saverne has a German garrison and they might well be alerted what is coming their way. You know the French. There are traitors everywhere in their ranks." He said the words without rancour. It was merely a statement of fact.

By eight, they were rolling through an area of what looked like market gardens, small houses set well apart, with large fields and glasshouses around them, which might well have supplied the prosperous cities of the plain with vegetables. Now, although there was smoke coming from the chimneys of the houses, there was no sign of life in the fields or the greenhouses. Obviously the small-holders had closed for the winter. Rory told himself this might be the very road they needed to circumvent Saverne. But soon he would realise he was mistaken – badly mistaken.

By nine, they were south of the Alsatian town. Here and there they passed civilians who stared at the

137

mud-splattered Jeeps filled with soldiers wearing an unfamiliar scarlet beret. But in the lead Mayne would smile and yell in his best German, *"Guten Tag, Guten Tag, mein Herr!"* in the hope that the civilians would take them for SS troops who wore similar camouflaged smocks to the SAS. In most cases it seemed to work, the stolid Alsatians would take off their caps as a mark of respect, and cry back, *"Guten Tag! Herr Offizier!"*

But while the Irish giant was all smiles in the presence of these civilians, his grey eyes were hard and wary, searching the hedges and fields to both sides for any sign of trouble. In his Jeep and in the ones following, the men aped their commander, waving and smiling at the civilians. But their weapons were already cocked and their trigger fingers were itchy, close to their pieces, ready to spring into action if necessary.

"Once in Italy last year," Corporal Stevens was saying, "I was caught in a mortar stonk and I jumped in a frigging hole for cover and do you know what – *it was full of shit!*"

Next to him at the back of Mayne's jeep, his running mate 'Tashy' Kennedy laughed. "Could only happen to you, Stevie! Fancy jumping into a hole full of crap! Don't know how you ever got into the SAS in the first frigging place." He shook his head sadly like a man sorely tried.

Mayne was only half listening to the usual banter that always took place between the two mates whenever they had a chance. He was a little nervous. They were bearing south-east all right, but they were still too close to Saverne and its Hun garrison for his liking. The weather was proving a blessing in one way. The low cloud was preventing any ground-spotting plane

138

from taking off from Saverne's military field. All the same, once the Germans became aware that something was happening in the Vosges, surely they would send out patrols into the foothills?

Suddenly Mayne was fully awake, every nerve tingling electrically. "Put out the anchors!" he hissed urgently at the driver.

Automatically and unquestioningly, the driver pressed hard on the brakes. The Jeep skidded to a stop, as behind Mayne's vehicle the other drivers did the same. Mayne bent down to his driver and hissed, as if he might well be overheard, "Back off nice and quietly. Don't rev too much."

The Jeep driver squirmed round in his seat and indicated that the drivers behind him should start moving back to give him room to reverse. Rory, to the rear, realised immediately that something had gone wrong. He indicated a field to their right. "In there," he called as loudly as he dared.

His driver took the iniative and drove carefully into the wet, soggy field, careful not to become bogged down. One by one the other Jeeps reversed into the same field, followed by Mayne's Jeep. Rory sprang out and doubled to where Mayne was now standing. "What is it?" he asked.

"Don't know exactly," Mayne said, somewhat puzzled. "Come on, Rory, I'll show you. But keep under cover. So far, I don't think they've spotted us."

Rory O'Sullivan couldn't guess who 'they' might be, but he asked no questions. Instead, he edged his way forward next to Paddy Mayne until they came to the bend again where Mayne had ordered his Jeep

139

driver to stop. "Don't use your glasses, Rory," Mayne ordered in a low voice, as they crouched. "The glint might give us away. OK, now what do you think?"

Rory bent and rubbed some of the wet earth on his face as a camouflage. Then, with his body at 45 degrees he lay full length on the wet cobbles, showing only his face, and peered to his front.

A primitive barrier had been erected across the little road. There was an old hay wagon and several railway sleepers, piled up to 6 ft high, and the whole ramshackled lot was guarded by a dozen or so civilians and it was clear that they were all armed.

"Now what do you make of that little lot?" Mayne asked grimly.

"Maquis?"

"Not likely with a German garrison perhaps only a mile or so away. Besides, these Alsatians are mostly pro-Hun, or so I've been told."

"Then who the hell are they?" Rory hissed in exasperation. They had come so far, now they were being stopped by a bunch of unknown armed civilians.

Mayne shook his big head. "I don't know, Rory. All I can tell you is that they're linked up to that other road," he indicated another road in the distance, where Rory could just make out a similar barrier. "For all I know yon civilians are barricading every road around Saverne and we, my lad, have got to do something about it pretty quick. Or General Leclerc is going to get a very bloody nose . . ."

PART THREE

End Run

Chapter One

Colonel Dio reacted immediately. Just as his Sherman, skidding and slithering in the snow, breasted the rise, he spotted it a – Boche 57mm gun dug in to the right of the mountain road. He didn't hesitate. "Enemy gun at two o'clock," he bellowed. "Gunner – fire!"

The Sherman's electrically operated turret swung round noiselessly. Without seeming to take aim, the gunner pressed his foot pedal. The Sherman's 75mm cannon belched fire in the very same instant that the German anti-tank gunners did the same.

The French gunner was more accurate, though. The shell slammed against the anti-tank gun's metal shield. There was the hollow boom of metal striking metal. Next moment the gun keeled over onto its side, scattering its crew in a mess of broken and severed limbs.

That first shot acted like a signal. Wild firing broke out from both sides of the road. Colonel Dio could hear the whine of the slugs as they howled off the thick metal hide of his tank. He prayed that the German ambushers were not armed with their dreaded one-shot rocket launchers, the *panzerfaust*.

Confined to this narrow road, with no room to dodge, the tanks were sitting ducks for the German infantry if they were armed with those killing tubes.

Dio made his decision. Somehow, he guessed, he had bumped into a small enemy outfit, perhaps reinforcements going up to the second-rate German division opposite the US 79th Division. He had to chance it, he knew that. Speed was of the essence. He didn't want to get bogged down in a slogging match up here. He spoke into his throat mike. "To all, keep going regardless of cost! *Vive la France!*"

Even as he gave his order, the Sherman behind him on the road staggered violently, rearing up on its rear bend like a wild horse being put to the saddle for the first time. It had been hit by a *panzerfaust* round. Next moment its vulnerable petrol engine went up in flames. Screaming, panicking men came tumbling out of the escape hatches as flames seared the deck like a gigantic blowtorch. They threw themselves into the snow, twisting and turning, trying to put out those greedy, killing flames.

Still the rest pressed on, the gunners firing wildly to left and right, their machine-guns chattering frantically, praying that they, too, would not be hit by one of those deadly missiles. In their half-tracks, the *poilus* crouched low, snapping off rifle shots to left and right, aiming at the rocks above them in case any *boche* attempted to drop grenades into the open decks of their vehicles.

Up front, Dio yelled through his throat mike again, "To all – *tempo – tempo!*" Below, his driver put his foot down harder on the accelerator, fighting the 30-ton monster as it skidded and slithered crazily in the wet snow. He knew what the commander wanted.

In the grey morning light, Colonel Dio caught the silver glint of an aerial to his left front. It would be the Germans means of communication with the rest of their division. "Gunner!" he cried urgently. "Radio aerial at two o'clock. Give it a burst of rapid!"

Again the gunner swung the turret round, as a missile hissed by the Sherman harmlessly, trailing angry red sparks behind it. He opened fire with his co-axial machine-gun. Tracer zipped lethally towards the communications group. The deadly burst scattered the Germans. Men went flying everywhere. One looked down at the front of his greatcoat, now stitched with red holes, in utter disbelief, as if he could not understand why this was happening to him.

As Colonel Dio's Sherman rolled by, the German's knees gave way beneath him like those of a new-born filly and he sank to the blood-red snow. And then they were through, rolling down the descent towards the Rhine plain, followed by frustrated fire, weakening by the second.

Twenty miles away at the chateau which he had selected for his command post for the first part of the operation, Leclerc, nervous and on edge as he always was at the start of an operation, listened carefully while his operations officers spelled out the details of Colonel Dio's fire-fight at the pass. "*Merci*," he said at the end of it, lighting yet another cigarette. "Anything else?"

The elegant staff officer looked a little worried. He hesitated.

"*Allez, Charles*," Leclerc urged. "Tell me, even if it's bad news, tell me!"

"The *rostbifs, mon general*," the other officer said. "They have been stopped on the outskirts of Saverne."

"The boche?" Leclerc asked urgently.

145

The other officer shrugged a little helplessly. "It is difficult, sir."

"Spit it out, man," Leclerc said.

"Well, we know the English are not a very intelligent race. It's all that tea, it addles their brains."

"Get on with it!"

"Well, sir, they seem to have been stopped by civilians. There has been no fighting as yet. But the *rostbifs* report there seem to be civilians at other road blocks in the area."

Leclerc frowned and stroked the ends of his trim, clipped moustache, as he always did when he was confused or had a problem. "Civilians, eh," he echoed. "But what could civilians be doing barricading roads when Saverne has a large German garrison?"

"Exactly, sir. The staff thought just the same. It can't be the Maquis, they'd never be allowed to get away with anything like that by the Boche." He shrugged again, a little frustrated that his trained staff mind could not solve the problem.

"But if it is not the Maquis," Leclerc said tonelessly in a low voice, almost as if speaking to himself, "who are these damned civilians?"

The staff officer remained silent. Outside, another squadron of tanks was moving off into the mountains. "*Bonne chance!*" someone was yelling above the noisy rattle of the Sherman's tracks. "The Boche are in the piss-pot now – shit on them!"

Despite his worries and feeling of uncertainty, Leclerc smiled to himself. It was the same statement that the commanding general of French troops surrounded at Sedan in 1870 had made. Now it was the Germans' turn. He made a decision. "Signal

146

the *rostbifs* immediately that they are to avoid a confrontation with these strange civilians. They are to make a detour *now* and find an undefended route from Saverne to Strasbourg for Colonel Dio."

The staff officer clicked to attention. *"Entendu, mon general,"* he cried before leaving the room. Leclerc, alone now, slumped in his chair and stared at the grey morning sky outside the tall 18th century window. He asked himself what the devil was going on down there at Saverne?

"Well?" Rory asked, after Stevens had read out Leclerc's message. "What now?"

Paddy Mayne rubbed his unshaven chin. "Well, I'll tell you this, I'm not going back into those bloody mountains. But I can't see how we can deploy any further without those civvie sods at the barricade seeing us. The fields ahead are wide open."

Rory frowned. Paddy Mayne was right. With a bit of luck the Jeeps, with their four-wheel drive, would be able to cross the muddy, sodden fields to the right of the barricade. But they'd be spotted immediately. Then all hell would break loose. All the same, he knew they couldn't hang around much longer where they were. Somebody would cotton on to them sooner or later. He sucked his front teeth thoughtfully before making up his mind. "Boss, I could make a diversion," he said a little hesitantly.

"What do you mean – a diversion?" Mayne snapped.

"I could make a dash for it across the fields to the left of the barricade, while you took the chaps round to the right."

147

Paddy Mayne shot him an angry look. "Have you blown a gasket or something?" he demanded. "I know all you Papists are soft in the head, but I didn't think you were that soft. You'd be for the chop once they spotted you."

Rory O'Sullivan returned the look in his own stubborn, hard manner. "Boss, I'm prepared to give it a try."

"But Rory," Mayne said in a more reasonable manner, "you're only 22, lad. You've got yer life before yer. Why throw it away needlessly? We've already lost one O'Sullivan in the SAS you know."

"There's plenty more where I come from," the younger officer maintained stoutly. "Besides, they've got to catch me first."

"You volunteer for this?" Mayne said formally and seriously. "And you too, Sergeant Smith?"

The big guardsman clicked to attention as if he were back on some pre-war barracks square. "I do, sir. Where Mr O'Sullivan goes, I go, as I did with the late Captain O'Sullivan."

"What a bloody family!" Mayne snorted, but there were tears in his eyes all the same. For the second time since they had come out of the mountains, Paddy Mayne was moved and Rory could see the strain he was under. He said, "Don't worry, Boss. We'll make it." He nodded to Smith.

Smith swung himself behind the wheel. Rory propped himself up in the seat next to him, flare pistol in his big hand. "All right, James!" he cried almost jauntily, "take her away and don't spare the horses!"

Smith started up. Next moment he had slipped across the road, lurched down and up out of the ditch

148

opposite and was jolting across the field to the left of the country road. Paddy Mayne shook his head, as if in sorrow, then he indicated that the drivers should be ready to move off immediately he gave the signal.

Now, Smith and O'Sullivan were in the middle of the field skidding and bumping between the two barricades. Rory said a quick prayer and raised his clumsy-looking signal pistol. He pressed the trigger and a flare shot into the grey sky. An second of so later it ignited with a soft plop to give a burst of red flame. At the barricade all eyes turned in the direction of the racing Jeep.

Fighting the wheel, Smith shouted above the roar of the racing engine, "May the Lord make us grateful for what we are about to receive!" He indicated the civilians already raising their weapons and pointing them in their direction.

"Amen to that," Rory replied equally solemnly. He prepared for what was soon to come, bracing himself for the first volley.

Nothing happened!

Suddenly the civilians were shouldering their weapons. They turned from the Jeep, fists were raised and there were angry shouts as if they might well be arguing among themselves. Rory flashed a look at the second barricade on the other road. The same thing was happening there. Indeed, some of the civilians were already abandoning the barricade and climbing into a gas-burning truck, which had arrived seemingly out of nowhere.

"That's a turn up for the book!" Smith yelled as they passed safely, heading again towards the road which led to Strasbourg. "What do you make of that, Boss?"

"God knows!" Rory had to admit. "But whatever made the civvies not fire saved our bacon all right."

Ten minutes later they were joined by the rest of the convoy, coming down to the road from the right, with Stevens in the rear already signalling Leclerc's HQ with Paddy Mayne's proud message. 'Sir, I am able to report the road is open. Strasbourg is yours. Goodbye!'

What was left of the 2nd SAS Regiment was on its way to settle a private score.

Chapter Two

Dr Barsch frowned, his fat face tightly screwed up, eyes closed as he tried to concentrate on his pleasure. The whore was expert and trying hard. She had her dyed blonde head between his legs working hard on him, sucking and pumping, but he simply couldn't become erect. His mind kept returning to the impending danger and the fact the damn-fool Professor had still not received permission from the *Reichsführer SS* Himmler for him to cross the Rhine with his precious collection.

He opened his eyes in the same moment that the whore, face flushed, took her lips away from his organ, saying, "I've tried my best, *Herr Doktor*. But it doesn't seem to work. Perhaps you're tired."

"Damn!" Barsch snapped angrily. "A man can't always just do his duty. A man ought to have a bit of pleasure."

The whore, who was going to be the last person to offend one of the most powerful men in Strasbourg, nodded her agreement. "Of course, *Herr Doktor*, of course." She gave him her fake whore's smile and thrusting out her plump, naked breasts, said, "Perhaps a jelly roll might do the trick, sir!"

"Ah, that's an idea," Barsch agreed and relaxed again, as she immersed his flaccid organ in the plump flesh, massaging her breasts so that a warm glow started to surge through his penis. "Good!" he breathed sharply. "Very good. Keep it up – I think you're going to do it this time, wench!"

Still smiling that practised whore's smile, she continued to kneed her breasts, wondering how much longer he was going to take. She had three more clients to service this midday, including the adjutant to the commanding general and he was a stickler for punctuality.

"Just a bit more now," Barsch gasped, mouth slack and gaping, a row of sweat beads gathering along his hair line. "Excellent . . . excellent . . . *Ja! Ja ich spritze . . . bald . . .!*"

Outside, a car skidded to a halt and a familiar voice bellowed at the sentry. "Get out of my way, man! You know full well who I am. Is Doctor Barsch in his office, damn you? It's important . . ." It was Chretien.

Barsch moaned, but not with pleasure. His erection disappeared rapidly and he said, "Get dressed. This is official. *Quick!*" Outside, he could hear Chretien pounding up the steps two at a time, obviously in a great hurry.

Flustered and worried, the whore started to put on her bra and blouse, while Barsch buttoned the flies of his breeches. He thrust a bundle of worthless notes into the whore's hand. "Will you be requiring me again this week?" she enquired, slipping into her coat.

"I dont know!" he snapped in irritation, all thoughts of sex had vanished. "Off you go – quick!"

He thrust her out of the office, just as a grim-faced Chretien, now in full uniform, with a machine-pistol slung over his shoulder, came to the head of the stairs.

152

He took the situation in at once. "Ah, the pleasures of the flesh, eh, Barsch! I'm afraid there will be little time for that now." He gave the blonde whore a cold look and she jiggled her rump at him as she went past.

"What do you mean?" Barsch asked urgently. "Trouble?"

"Yes, lot's of it."

Barsch's pudgy face turned white with fear. He sat down abruptly. Chretien unslung his machine-pistol and said in that harsh, demanding manner of his, "Give me a drink, Barsch, I damn well need one."

Obediently, not even offended by the manner in which Chretien had asked for his usual cognac, Barsch shoved the bottle of Asbach Uralt towards him.

"German hooch!" Chretien sneered. "Ah well better than nothing." He raised the bottle to his lips and took a deep swig of the fiery German brandy. Then he coughed throatily and slammed the bottle down on Barsch's desk, hard, as if he were controlling himself only with difficulty.

Impatiently, Barsch waited for him to speak, though he knew whatever news the Alsatian would bring would be unpleasant.

"Everything's gone wrong at Saverne," Chretien announced.

"How do you mean?"

"That fool of an agent of mine with the Reds has gone and got himself caught. Apparently the Reds had been trailing him for days. At all events, they knocked him about a bit and he deserved it," Chretien added bitterly. "Stupid swine not seeing an obvious tail – and he sang like a canary. Result?" He shrugged angrily, "They called off their people at the barricades around

153

Saverne. Probably they thought it was a put-up job on our part. Hell, it doesn't matter now. All that does matter is that the way is wide open for Leclerc once he gets out of the mountains, the scum." He reached for the bottle and took another deep, angry slug of the cognac.

"What about the garrison at Saverne?" Barsch asked a little helplessly.

"Cardboard soldiers!" Chretien snorted. "Ear and stomach battalions*, young kids still wet behind the spoons, old syphilitic pricks who can hardly hold a rifle. Christmas tree soldiers, the whole shitting lot of them!"

"What can be done?" Barsch asked.

"I've been thinking about that," Chretien said, his angry mood vanishing, to be replaced by one of thoughtfulness. "If we can't hold these Tommies at Saverne, we could still stop them on the road to Strasbourg. That could delay Leclerc sufficiently long for our troops to come over the Rhine and deal with them."

Barsch grasped at straws. The word "delay" impinged upon his brain. Any "delay" might well mean that he would receive the movement order in time so that he could do a bunk before the balloon went up. "Do we know which road the Tommies are using?" he asked eagerly.

"No," Chretien answered. "But we can soon find out if you can authorise a spotter plane."

"*Gesagt – getan* – said one," Barsch answered, using the old German phrase. "When?"

---

* Battalions formed from men suffering from ear and stomach complaints, who would receive special diets, etc.

"Now, if possible, before the next snow shower."

Barsch picked up the telephone on his desk. "Give me the commandant of Fort Ney, operator," he demanded. While he waited, he held his hand over the mouthpiece and whispered, "I got him off a rather serious racial charge. He had been consorting with a Yiddish wench. I saw he was cleared, though, of course," he added, as if it was the most obvious thing in the world, "we had to send her up the chimney." He made a circling motion with his forefinger to symbolise smoke rising from the gas ovens.

"It was the best way of getting rid of the, er, incriminating evidence." He smiled at Chretien. "The man owes me a favour – Oh, yes. Major, you still have your own spotter plane, I believe?" He listened attentively, before saying, "I'm afraid I can't let you have the details, top secret, you understand. But I need a plane and pilot urgently. For about —" he turned to Chretien for guidance.

"The rest of this afternoon."

Barsch repeated the words, then snapped, "*Danke Herr Major*. I shall mention your kind assistance in my report, never fear." He slammed the phone down. "Well, you've got your plane Chretien. You don't need me I suppose?"

"No," the other man agreed. "Just write me up the necessary permission for this Jew-loving friend of yours and I'll be off. You stay and prepare whatever forces you can gather for the trouble to come."

"Of course, of course," Barsch agreed hastily, as he scribbled out the required permission on the official form. He wanted rid of Chretien as soon as possible.

155

Also, he needed to go and see that damned Professor once more, urgently.

Chretien grabbed the form and said, "For now on, Barsch, it's march or croak."

Barsch assumed his martial air, his "war face number one", as he always called it to himself. "*Marschieren oder kreperien*, you're right there, Chretien."

Hastily, the Alsatian slung his machine-pistol over his shoulders and went out.

Barsch waited until he had gone. Then he sneered, to himself, "Yes, my foolish friend, you *croak*, and I *march*, home to mother." Next moment he had picked up his own cap and was gone, too.

It had begun to snow again. For once, Paddy Mayne was glad of it. Driving was easier here on the plain than in the High Vosges and the snow gave them the cover they needed. Once they had passed a small group of German soldiers, but before the enemy could realise that they were British, the little convoy of Jeeps had vanished into the snowstorm. Otherwise the villages, mostly a collection of medieval half-timbered houses grouped around an onion-topped church seemed deserted as they passed through them, though Mayne suspected that the villagers were listening tensely behind locked doors and shutters.

About midday, after they had stopped briefly for a brew-up and a slab of bully beef on a hard ration biscuit they heard the plane. The ceiling was low and they couldn't see the aircraft. Instinctively, however, they knew it spelled danger. "Ay," Sergeant Smith commented to Rory, as he tried to pierce the whirling white gloom, "yon bugger is out looking for us, yer can bet yer boots on that!"

Rory nodded and knew that Smithie was right. By now the Germans would know that Leclerc had broken through; the enemy was always very expert in intercepting radio traffic and tankers tended to communicate a lot with one another over their radios. It stood to reason that their planes would be out looking for the point of Leclerc's advance.

After a while, the plane droned away and they continued their advance, each man wrapped in a cocoon of his own fears and worries. For all of them knew that Strasbourg was heavily garrisoned by the Germans, based on the many fortresses – Foch, Petain, Ney and the like – which protected the Alsatian capital. As Paddy had told him during the last brew-up: "We know where the Gestapo HQ is, in the *Place Kleber*. That's where that bastard Dr Barsch will be no doubt. But we can't hang about, asking too many question. It's going to be a shoot, snatch and scoot op, Rory my boy."

He had known what Paddy meant. They'd have to take the Germans by surprise, grab their man and do a bunk in so many minutes. They could not chance being bogged down in a long-winded shoot-out. German superiority would be too great; they wouldn't stand a chance. But risky as the operation was, Rory felt certain that all the men were behind it. They all wanted revenge on the man who had tortured their dead comrades so cruelly.

The return of the plane caught them completely by surprise. They had just emerged from one of the Rhenish villages when it came hurtling towards them out of the snow storm at virtually tree-top height. Despite the snow, they could see the white blurs of the pilot's and his observer's faces and there was no mistaking that hard black and white German cross. *"Knock the bugger out of the sky!"* Mayne yelled at the top of his voice and, standing up in his seat, blazed away furiously with his Colt. Behind the lead Jeep, gunners swung their twin Brownings upwards and started filling the air with a wall of lethal tracer.

But it was too late. The Germans had seen all they wanted to. The pilot jerked back the stick. The little monoplane rose sharply into the whirling white sky. Moments later it had disappeared into the storm, with a triumphant Chretien already radioing details of what he had seen back to Fort Ney.

"Well, that's frigging well torn it," Mayne cursed to no one in particular. "They've spotted us all right." Angrily, he thrust the smoking Colt back into its holster and considered what they should do next now that the Germans were aware of their coming. They wouldn't need a crystal ball to figure out that this was the point of Leclerc's armour, now presumably heading in the general direction of Saverne. How would they react?

As the little convoy rolled on, Paddy Mayne racked his brains in trying to out-think the enemy. Would they ambush this road? Or would they concentrate on defending Strasbourg itself? He guessed they wouldn't have the troops and resources to defend the whole of Strasbourg, the place was too big and the defence of large cities ate up infantry divisions. With the Germans under attack all along the 500-mile long Western Front, they simply couldn't spare the troops.

He made his decision. Leclerc was on his own now. He could take care of himself. No ambush would stop his 30-ton Shermans for long; but it would stop the SAS's unarmoured Jeeps. So the answer was to get off this road, where the Germans had spotted them and find some sort of alternative. He flashed a look to his right. The fields were white and heavy with snow and the Jeeps with their four-wheel drive would find it difficult to get across them. At the best their progress would be painfully slow.

Then he had it! *Hostages*!

Chapter Three

It was clear that the Germans were moving back in disorder. In the snowy field to their right, there was an abandoned German tank-destroyer, one track stretched behind it like a severed limb. Beyond it there was a truck, its windscreen broken and with both its rear tyres burst. In their haste to escape, the fleeing Germans had left the truck's engine running. Now the motor throbbed on uselessly, with the dead driver slumped over the wheel.

Rory and Paddy Mayne crouched at the edge of the village and watched the scene, looking eagerly for what they sought. Obviously this rabble was fleeing before Leclerc's advance. But the garrison troops from Strasbourg would be more organised and disciplined than the leaderless group of Germans milling around in the centre of the village square; and it would be the Strasbourg troops who would attempt to stop them.

"Not what you'd call your Brigade of Guards," Paddy Mayne said contemptuously as he watched a skinny runt of a soldier with glasses knock the neck off a bottle of looted beer and drink the contents greedily. Next to him, another puny *landser* in a mud-stained ankle-length greatcoat squatted on the kerb, dejected, his head sunk into his hands, as if he hadn't the strength to drink the looted *Mutzig Pils*.

160

"Suits me, Boss," Rory said. "Easy pickings with that little lot of deadbeats."

"Exactly."

The snow-storm was letting up now and Paddy Mayne knew he needed its cover if he was going to get into the village, seize his hostages and do a bunk before the Huns knew what had hit them. He looked to left and right where his frozen troopers crouched, their camouflage smocks white with snow.

He liked what he saw. Despite the conditions and the danger, his men looked hard and determined. He signalled left and right. Noiselessly, hardly making a sound in the snow, his troopers moved forward on both flanks as Paddy got to his feet. "All right, you Rory, here's where we do our Hun officer act."

The SAS never wore helmets in action, but their paras' helmets were very similar to those worn by the Germans. Now Mayne and O'Sullivan put on their helmets and started to march through the snow to the village square. They did so quite boldly, aping that arrogance of their caste which they had seen in German officers. No one paid any attention to them. The fugitives continued to drink the beer that they had looted from the local inn until Paddy Mayne chanced his arm and bellowed, "*Grussen Sie nicht wenn Sie einen Offizier sehen!*"

A couple of them sprang to attention, the old iron-hard Prussian discipline reasserting itself, and saluted.

Casually Mayne returned their salute and marched on with a lordly mien on his craggy unshaven face.

"Christ, Boss, you chanced your arm there," Rory whispered out of the side of his mouth.

161

Mayne grinned. "Well, one has to live up to the old regimental motto – He who dares and all that. They'll be talking about this in the regimental mess in 50 years time. We'll be legends."

"*Dead bloody legends!*" a harsh little voice at the back of Rory's head said coldly. Aloud, Rory O'Sullivan said, "Look at that military sign post, Boss."

Mayne looked at the myriad signboards tacked to a telephone pole. They were the usual rash of army abbreviations understood only by soldiers. "What about it?"

"That one with the red cross, Boss. Must be a field dressing station or a casualty clearing place. There could be nurses, female nurses there," he added significantly, knowing Paddy Mayne's plan.

The big Ulsterman got it immediately. "Rory, you're not just a pretty face. Exactly right for what we intend." He looked to right and left. Like grey ghosts his troopers were keeping pace with them in the side streets on either side. Everything was going to plan. "Come on!"

They followed the direction indicated by the Red Cross sign and the word '*Hauptverbandplatz*'*. They turned a corner and then they saw it. A house much larger than the others in the village, perhaps that of some rich businessman who commuted to Strasbourg. Outside in the cobbled courtyard, there were two battered German ambulances, both showing the scars where they had been hit by bullets, next to a pile of weapons abandoned by the wounded inside.

* Main Dressing Station.

An old civilian trudged by the ambulances, carrying a severed leg and an arm in a bucket. Perhaps he was the caretaker. He paid no attention to the two strangers. Mayne nodded to Rory. "This is. Let's get cracking," he whispered.

Boldly, they walked through the front entrance, nostrils assailed by the stink of human ordure, ether and suffering. On both sides of the corridor lay wounded soldiers. A few were unconscious. But most of them slumped there apathetically or lay moaning softly, clutching the bloody paper bandages that had been bound around their wounds.

At the end of the corridor they hesitated, wondering which way to go. Then to their left they spotted a heavy-bosomed nurse, a mask over her mouth and dressed in a blood-stained white rubber apron and boots. "Operating theatre," Mayne mouthed the words "There's our nurses." They hurried on.

They flung open the door. A surgeon, his apron stained with blood from top to bottom, was sawing through a leg bone, while a nurse carefully dabbed the sweat from his brow.

Rory gritted his teeth at the sound of the saw grinding through the bone, which looked like polished ivory in a sea of red gore.

Suddenly the surgeon saw them. He looked questioningly over his mask. The nurse stopped patting his brow and turned to stare at the intruders. "*Was wollen —* " the muffled words died on her lips as she saw the big Colts which had appeared in both men's fists as if by magic.

The surgeon hesitated. Then he decided he had to do his duty first, as Mayne, jerking up his pistol, indicated he was their prisoner. Hurriedly he applied the saw to the bone once more, the instrument making a sickening grating sound. An instant later he was through. He dropped the saw and accepted the scalpel which the nurse had thrust into his hand. With a deft turn of his wrist, he severed the rest of the leg. It dropped with a squelch to the blood-slippery floor. "What do you want?" he asked in weary, accented English, as the sister began to sew up the gaping wound.

"You, doctor," Mayne answered in a voice noticeably quieter than usual. "We need you and the nurses."

"Me? What for?"

"Don't ask question, doctor. Just do as you are told."

At that moment Tashy came into the makeshift operating theatre. "Everything all right, Boss," he reported. "We've got the place covered."

"Thanks, Tashy," his C.O. snapped. "Tell the drivers to bring up the Jeeps. We're going in five minutes."

"Will do, sir," Tashy replied, eyeing the massive bosom of one of the German nurses. "Turned out nice agen," he said to no one in particular and then he was gone.

"We're taking you with us, doctor," Mayne informed the surgeon, who spoke English. "You're going to be our protection!"

"Protection against what?" the German interrupted him.

Mayne didn't enlighten him. "Just let me say that as soon as we reach Strasbourg, we shall let you and the others go. We have nothing against you. It might be a blessing in disguise for you," he added. "At least you'll be able to get across the Rhine in time before the French arrive because then there'll be trouble if I know the French. All right, take what you need. Let's get going."

"But the Geneva Convention states — " the surgeon began to bluster, but Paddy cut him short with an angry, "When did the bloody Germans pay any heed to the Geneva Convention?" He jerked up the muzzle of his Colt threateningly. "OK, let's move it."

Five minutes later they were on their way again. In the lead Jeep with Paddy Mayne and the driver there were the surgeon and one of his nurses, still clad in the white rubber overalls of the surgery and with the dressing station's Red Cross flag draped across the Jeep's bonnet. Behind, each of the other Jeeps carried one member of the hospital staff in their easily recognisable white uniforms.

As Paddy Mayne had stated just before they had set off once more, "Lads, I don't think even the Huns would attack us with their own people being used by us as hostages. Fire at us and the Huns will take the same stick. Strasbourg here we come!"

As the spotter plane came back, buzzing the little convoy, Rory told himself that he hoped the C.O. was right. He, personally, wouldn't trust the average Hun as far as he could throw him. But Tashy Kennedy, pressed up tightly against the buxom nurse in the narrow confines of his Jeep, was very happy with the situation. As he felt the frightened woman's massive right breast thrust warmly into his arm, despite the white uniform, he told himself joyfully, "Now this is what I call going to war in sodding style!"

165

The little convoy now bowled along in fine style. The weather had cleared in front, and next to the scowling German surgeon, who had lapsed into a sulky silence, Paddy Mayne thought that the very air was warmer. He guessed they were coming to that great river, the Rhine, which divided France from Germany.

Here and there they passed little groups of German stragglers. Some were armed, others had flung away their weapons in their panicky haste to escape the advancing French. They let the Jeeps by without hindrance, not even particularly interested, or it seemed, in the fact that there were Germans with these foreign soldiers.

Paddy Mayne thought that was a good sign. As they rolled by yet another group of dispirited German troops, still armed with a couple of Spandaus, he told himself that they were going to make it without a fight. But as was often the case in his chequered army career, which had seen him nearly court-martialled twice, Paddy was wrong. As they drove by a road sign bearing the legend '*Strassburg 18 KL*', he heard the first faint but definite squeaky rattle of tank tracks to his front. With a sinking feeling the giant Ulsterman told himself the only tanks in front of them were German!

Chapter Four

Dr Barsch was scared. As he drove to the university everything seemed very normal. People were standing in line waiting for their rations outside the butchers, soldiers strode purposefully down the streets, an officer, obviously from the staff, cantered along taking his daily ride, whores waited in doorways. Strasbourg seemed as it had always been, a large provincial city well behind the front.

Barsch knew differently. The news had just come in to his office that Saverne had been taken by a *coup de main*. Leclerc's French had caught the garrison completely by surprise. Hundreds of German troops, perhaps thousands, had been taken without firing a single shot. The French had even captured two German generals sitting behind their writing desks, signing orders as if the war was hundreds of kilometres away. Now it was obvious that the French were heading for Strasbourg hell-for-leather.

His driver swung by the *Pont de Kehl*, the main bridge across the Rhine, linking Strasbourg with Kehl on the German side. Traffic flowed across it, as it had always done. These days, now that Alsace was German again, there were no customs men to hinder the smooth flow of traffic. In the rear seat Barsch looked longingly at the far side. That narrow stretch of water was all that separated him from the Reich and safety. He licked his suddenly dry lips. Should he just order his driver to turn and cross the bridge? For a moment he was tempted. But he knew what would happen to him if he was caught, especially now when the city was likely to become part of the battle zone. The Field Security Police would shoot him out of hand without trial for having deserted. No, that was too risky. He needed an official order to cross: something which would give him time to find a new identity and the requisite documents. Then he could take a dive and become a 'U-boat', as the saying had it. He'd go underground and sit out the rest of the war until it was safe enough to surface once more.

Even in his present state of panic, Dr Barsch, the trained historian and former schoolmaster, reasoned that the Western Allies wouldn't keep a conquered Germany oppressed for ever. Germany was too big and they would need the defeated Reich to help them in the coming struggle against Soviet Russia. Sooner or later everything would return to normal. But somehow he had to *survive* that long.

Now they started to approach the university and Dr Barsch's nervousness increased. He had already prepared what he was to say to the fool of a professor. Now everything was muddled in his head. The driver started to slow down. To left and right the students, mostly female and in uniform, threw up their right hands and greeted him with "*Heil Hitler!*" Routinely, he returned their salutes, even ignoring the tall blonde with the pouting lips who gave him a significant 'come hither' look. His mind was concentrated solely on his problem. Then he realised that this day might well be the turning point of his life. If he fell into the hands of the French, he knew absolutely, he wouldn't live long. They would show no mercy to an SD officer who had fought the *Resistance* for nearly three years.

He got out of the car and started down the corridor to the professor's department. Self-important lecturers, most of them in SA or SS uniform, went by him, saluting rigidly as they tucked in their fat bellies and attempted to look like soldiers. Again he returned their salutes automatically, preoccupied with his own problem.

The professor's fat secretary, whom Barsch suspected supplied the former with whatever sexual services he needed, clicked to attention behind her desk with a deep, masculine *"Heil Hitler"*, followed by "The *Herr Professor* is expecting you. Please go straight through."

He nodded his acknowledgement and went through the door into the long hall where the fat fool kept his specimens.

The professor had his back to him, peering into a glass container at something which Barsch couldn't see for the man's bulk. He cleared his throat and the professor spun round, crying, *"Mein lieber Herr Doktor Barsch,* how good of you to come and see me in my, er —" He grinned, revealing a mouthful of gold teeth – "ivory tower."

Barsch nodded and opened his mouth to speak. The professor beat him to it. "Just look at it," he chortled, extending his pudgy right hand to the glass container. "The start of a new collection!"

Barsch stared hard at the container, a faint sense of nausea threatening to overcome him again. A black head stared back at him through the turgid umbalming fluid.

"The first of my new collection. Negroid types, one hundred per cent black blood and those adulterated by white blood of perverted Americans."

"What?" Barsch asked in a choked voice. He still couldn't get used to the fat fool's pickled bits and pieces of human beings.

"The *Reichsführer SS* has ordered," the professor answered proudly, puffing out his chest, "now that I have finished my Jewish collection, to begin one on the black race. In Italy we've got all sorts of the black degenerates fighting against us – Basuto, West Africans, Berbers and so on. They are going to be shipped, those we *apprehend*, here for me. This specimen came from a dead prisoner taken at the front mear Metz. It's in very good condition, a good example of a white-black mixture. Look at the cranium and the lips, which aren't typical negroid — "

"*Herr Professor,*" Barsch interrupted frantically. "You have spoken with the *Reichsführer*?"

"Yes," the other man said quite casually, while Barsch clenched his fists so tightly that it hurt. "Late yesterday evening just after I had given my lecture on 'Runic Symbols and the Germanic Creed'."

"What did he say?" Barsch asked desperately.

"Say about what?"

"Say about saving your collection – for the Reich?" Barsch stuttered, trying to control himself, the sweat running unpleasantly down the small of his back. He would have liked to have struck the stupid man with his "collections". The world was falling apart and he still thought he could play his little academic games.

170

The professor beamed at him winningly. "Good that you reminded me of that *Herr Doktor*. I had meant to telephone you, but I must confess the matter slipped my mind. I've been so taken up by this new collection which the *Reichsführer* had suggested. What a challenge! It will occupy me, I am sure, until I have to relinquish my chair — "

"WHAT DID HE SAY?" Barsch bellowed in the same tone he had used so often on frightened schoolboys and later on on even more frightened prisoners. "AM I TO TAKE THE COLLECTION BACK TO THE REICH OR NOT, MAN?"

The professor looked slightly puzzled at the change in Barsch's tone, but he accepted it without question. "Oh yes," he answered. "Just in case."

"Just in case, what?" Barsch's face turned puce with suppressed rage. "Please!"

"Just in case there should be any trouble here," the fat fool rambled on, "though of course both I and the *Reichsführer* don't expect anything to happen. However, it is best to plan for the worse, as my dear friend Himmler said."

At Barsch's right temple a nerve started to tick furiously. He was losing control of himself.

"Well, the *Reichsführer* has made his decision." The professor beamed at Barsch. "You, *Herr Doktor* are to take charge of the collection, supply the vehicles and escort to see that this unique material is taken in safety to Rastatt on the other side of the Rhine."

Barsch was no longer listening to the old fool. All energy seemed to have drained from his body. It was as if a tap had been opened and it had all vanished.

171

He was saved – *saved*! "When?" he heard himself ask weakly, his voice appearing to come from a long way off.

"*Reichsführer* Himmler suggested dawn tomorrow."

Barsch could have cheered. In less than 24 hours he would be on the other side of the Rhine. Suddenly his feeling of contempt for the fat professor vanished. He was a good man, a very good man. Unwittingly he had done him, Barsch, a great service. "I will be ready then, *Herr Professor*."

"I, too. You and your people will load up and as *Reichsführer SS* told me, you should reach Rastatt before those enemy air gangsters take to the skies over the Reich." He looked at Barsch very seriously. "After all, nothing must be allowed to happen to the collection." He raised one pudgy forefinger, like a hairy pork sausage, as if he were making an important point to his students in one of his lectures. "For undoubtedly it will become one of the greatest medical records in the Reich. People will be talking about the collection long after we are gone, my dear Barsch. Now there is work to be done." He clicked to attention and threw up his right arm in the German greeting – "*Heil Hitler*!"

"*Heil Hitler*!"

Dr Barsch went out as if treading on air. When here and there one of the uniformed students saluted, he returned the salute in great style, beaming at the younger person. His mind raced, it took only a phone call or two and he would have the needed trucks; the power of the Gestapo still held sway in Strasbourg. The escort would be his own trusted men. Just like he did, they knew their lives would come to a short

172

and brutal end if they were captured by the French on this side of the Rhine.

"*Heil Hitler, Hauptsturmbannführer* Barsch" – a sweet, demure young voice broke into his reverie.

He turned, startled by the use of his name.

A girl stood there, a pale blonde with serious blue eyes, clad in the black and white uniform of the Hitler Maidens. She didn't look a day over 14, but she had breasts all right, little things that tilted against the thin white material of her uniform blouse. "Do I know you?" he asked hesitantly, peering at her through his pince-nez.

"Yes, *Hauptsturm*," she said and gave a pretty curtsey, blushing a little. "My father served under you and when he was shot in the winter you were kind enough to pay your respects at the funeral."

"Ah, yes, I recall now. You dear father fell in action for Folk, Fatherland and Führer. He was sadly missed." In reality, Barsch told himself, her father *Scharführer* Ahrens was a drunken, lecherous swine, who had been shot in the back by one of his comrades when he had tried to seduce the latter's wife.

"Thank you," Fraulein Ahrens said sweetly. "You are very kind, sir."

"Not so formal," he said smiling at her winningly. Across his mind's eye there flashed those delightful images of his years as a young teacher when he would lean over one of his girl pupils, seemingly wanting to encourage her. In reality he had tried to peer down at the girls' little breasts or he had put his arm round them and had given them a supposedly playful squeeze. Those had been good, innocent days, he told himself.

173

Suddenly it came to him. "I have been recalled for duty to the Reich, Fraulein Ahrens. I know you can't stay out late, but I would be more than delighted if you could spend the rest of this afternoon with me. We could talk about you dear, dead father. Perhaps I could treat you to something nice." He licked his lips, as if he were preparing to enjoy a special meal, which in a way he was. He looked down at the pale blonde hopefully.

"*Naturlich, Sturmbannführer.*" Again she curtseyed. "I would be delighted." Like a sheep being led away to slaughter, she went with him to the waiting car. At the wheel the driver saw the two of them approaching in his rear view mirror. "Shit on shingle," he said to himself, nipping out his cigarette swiftly – Dr Barsch was very strict about smoking in his official car – "the old slime shitter's up to his games agen!"

174

Chapter Five

"Cor ferk a duck!" Smith exclaimed as the little Jeep convoy came to a halt. "What a frigging performance!"

On the hill to their right, the first tank had just breasted the rise and rolled to a stop.

Rory flung up his glasses. "Assault gun, one of those Renaults the Frogs make for the Huns."

"Don't care if it's a bleeding Rolls Royce, Boss," Smith retorted. "It looks bleeding dangerous to me."

Now, two more of the assault guns had appeared. Behind them a gas-burning truck also came up, the rear packed with riflemen in the blue uniform of the *Millice*. They, too, stopped and Rory caught the glint of glass as someone on the other side focused his binoculars on the SAS men.

Rory acted promptly. "Stand up . . . *Aufstehen!*" he rasped at their prisoner.

Miserably, as if he were about to be put in front of a firing squad, the little bespectacled doctor, in his blood-stained white apron, got to his feet. In the other Jeeps his fellow hostages were being forced to do the same.

Up front, Mayne waited tensely. What would the Huns do?

No one moved on both sides, as the two groups of

enemies considered their positions. Mayne knew the only chance he stood against the three assault guns was to make smoke and run for it if it came to a fight. Yet he still hoped that, now the enemy had seen their comrades who were their prisoners, it wouldn't come to that.

On the hill, Chretien raged inwardly as the two German artillery officers, both in their thirties with their chests covered in decorations, indicating that they had seen plenty of action, deliberated. Why were they taking all this time, he cursed to himself. Leclerc's tanks were already through Saverne. There might still be a chance of holding if they wiped out these *rostbifs* who were Leclerc's ears and eyes, at least long enough for fresh troops and tanks to be sent across the Rhine at Kehl.

The little *Oberleutnant* with the patch over his left eye was saying, "Those medics the Tommies are holding don't stand a chance if we open fire. All right, it's against the rules of land warfare. But that's the way the situation is. On has to be realistic about these things."

His fellow officer, tall and lean with the Knight's Cross of the Iron Cross hanging from his neck by its black and white ribbon, nodded as if he agreed entirely. "Yes, *Herr Kamerad*, you are right. We can't open fire on them, but all the same, we can't allow them to proceed any further, you know."

Chretien's hard, scarred face lit up. "Why bother about a few sawbones and lesbian nurses, all nurses are lesbian, everyone knows that," he said contemptuously. "There are bigger things at stake than their pitiful little lives." Hurriedly, he filled the two German officers in on the details of Leclerc's drive, ending with, "If you don't stop them this day, we lose Strasbourg, perhaps even the war."

The taller of the two officers said, "Perhaps you are making too much of this." He looked at the officer with the black eye patch. "What do you think?"

"I think," the other man said, giving him a crooked smile, "that we ought to buy combs. There are lousy times ahead."

The tall officer smiled faintly at the old soldier's expression. "Nothing we can do then?"

The other man shook his head. "But to please this gentleman," he indicated a fuming Chretien, "we can halt here and prevent their further progress. If and when this Frenchman Leclerc appears then we have done our duty and can retire gracefully, honour satisfied."

"Agreed. That is what we will do then," the tall officer said.

Two hundred yards away, Smith breathed, "Well, they've not opened fire yet, Boss. That's something."

"Yes," Rory agreed. "But they are making no signs of moving. We're wasting precious time waiting here like this and twiddling our damned thumbs."

"Thank God we've still got thumbs to twiddle," was Smith's cheerful reply.

"Amen to that," Rory agreed.

Up front, Paddy Mayne wasn't so sanguine. Time was of the essence. He was sure that the authorities in Strasbourg would already know, or soon would, that Leclerc had broken through the High Vosges. Those with anything to fear like the unknown Dr Barsch would be doing a bunk at the first

177

possible opportunity. If they were going to catch the swine, they had to keep moving. Every hour counted.

Grimly he stared at the three German assault guns blocking the way. They hadn't opened fire, obviously his dodge with the hostages had worked, but neither had they moved. What was he to do?

He knew that each Jeep team carried magnetic grenades, which could be clamped to armour to explode with a devasting effect. But how could he get a grenade crew underway without his troopers being spotted by the Germans on the heights? He frowned.

Behind him at the radio, Stevens sang out cheerfully, "It's a bastard, muvver, and so are you, son!"

It was an old army phrase intended to cheer up the Irish giant, but it didn't work the trick with Mayne. Grumpily he snapped: "No more bloody inane remarks like that, Stevie! Anything from this Frog Colonel Dio Yet?"

"Not a sausage sir," Stevens began, somewhat subdued. "But the air's full of static and German brass bands banging away." He meant the usual German device of blotting out enemy communications between units. "The Jerries know the balloon's gone up —"

He broke off suddenly. "Here they come, sir. It's the *Milice*. They're bloody well doing a frigging bayonet charge!"

Chretien's nerve had snapped, he had listened to the two Germans long enough. His face full of contempt, he had sneered, "What in three devils' names is the German Army, a shitting debating club? *Do something!*" And when the two artillery officers had shrugged and asked, "What do you suggest we do,

178

Major?", he had snarled back, "I'll show you what we will do. We Alsatians, are not afraid to die for the cause." He had turned to his *Milice*, all hard-bitten veterans of the year-long battle against the Maquis. "Comrades," he had shouted, "Fix bayonets!"

Now as both the Germans and the SAS watched in amazement, the blue-uniformed *Miliciens* came running down the hill, bayonets fixed, their NCOs yelling encouragement,their officers shrilling their whistles. It was like a scene from an old World War One movie.

The SAS raised their weapons. Behind their twin machine-guns, the gunners were ready to open fire at command. Mayne raised his hand. "Don't fire!" he yelled above the racket made by the French. His face revealed his doubts. If he opened fire at the French what would the German assault gunners do? Would they support the *Milice* and risk killing their own people. What the hell was he to do?

It was Tashy Kennedy who involuntarily made his decision for him. The buxom nurse next to him tried to bury her ample body in the bottom of the Jeep, terrified as she was of the charging troops. Her rump struck the SAS trooper on the right arm and his trigger finger jerked backwards involuntarily. A stream of white tracer zipped across the field towards the *Milice*.

Suddenly everyone was joining in, carried away by that blind and unreasoning blood lust of war, pumping shot after shot at the *Milice*. Frenchmen went down everywhere, bowled over by the impact of the bullets, all flailing arms and legs. Still they came on, their ranks thinner now. Mayne, who knew that his troopers were temporarily out of control, not listening to his

179

repeated shouts of "*Cease fire! Cease damned firing! will ye!*" tensed, waiting for the first throaty crunch of the assault guns opening up. Nothing happened. The German gunners didn't fire.

And then the gasping, choking *Milice*, what was left of them, were crossing the road and at their head was an evil-looking, scar-faced officer, already bleeding from a head wound. Mayne knew he had to stop them. He raised his Colt and took deliberate aim, as if back on some peacetime range. Taking his time, telling himself he could not miss, he took first pressure, relaxed his breathing and then pulled the trigger back gently. The big pistol bucked slightly in his great fist as Colts always did. He didn't miss.

The officer paused in mid-stride, a sudden puzzled look on his face. He seemed to remain there for an age. Then slowly, very slowly, as his pistol clattered to the ground from suddenly nerveless fingers, he sank to the road, while all around him the survivors began tossing away their weapons and raising their hands in reluctant surrender.

"See what you can do for the wounded," Mayne ordered the German doctor, still keeping his grey eyes fixed on the assault guns in the ridge. Suddenly he started. There was the throaty wheezing sound of a tank engine being turned on. "Christ!" Mayne exclaimed. "That's torn it!"

But as the German medics swarmed out to help the wounded the best they could without equipment, the first assault gun started to pull back, its long overhanging barrel cranked lower, as tanks always do when they travel.

"Well," Sergeant Smith cried, pushing his maroon

beret to the back of his head as if in bewilderment, "you can blow me down with a feather. The Jerries are backing off."

They certainly were. As the first one disappeared back over the ridge, there was a tremendous banshee-like howl, followed by what sounded like canvas being ripped apart. Next instant a shell exploded on the ridge line in a burst of angry red flame. That did it, the remaining two assault guns turned tail and scuttled for cover; the advancing French were ranging in on them. Leclerc was coming.

Ten minutes later, Chretien died, but not before he had talked to the German surgeon, who acted as Paddy Mayne's interpreter. Gravely wounded as he was the *Milicien* remained as bitter as he had always been. "We've shot your people all over eastern France," he said, breath coming in shallow gasps. "I . . . I recognise the badge." He tried to indicate the winged dagger badge of the SAS but was too weak to do so.

Paddy Mayne's heart skipped a beat. "Do you know a Dr Barsch?" he asked the dying man carefully, through the interpreter.

Chretien nodded, his face contorted with both pain and bitterness. "Yes, I know the yellow swine. Now he'll try to save his skin before . . . before you get to Strasbourg." Chretien coughed and a thin trickle of deep red blood ran from the side of his mouth. The surgeon patted it away with his handkerchief and shook his head helplessly.

"Where will he be?" Mayne asked carefully, noting how waxen and pinched the wounded man's nose had become. It was a sure sign that he was dying.

181

"Gestapo HQ," Chretien said weakly. "*Kaiserpalast.*" With one last supreme effort Chretien sat up and said, his mouth full of blood, "If you catch him, string him up by the pen —" He didn't finish his death wish. Abruptly, he fell backwards, dead.

Five minutes, leaving the medics behind, the little convoy was on its way once more. Now they drove at a speed. Barsch would not escape.

"String him up by the balls," Smith said grimly, as he hunched over the wheel. "That's what that dead Frog told the Boss. That'll be too good for him after what he did to our lads."

Rory O'Sullivan nodded his agreement and flashed a glance at the sign-post as they dashed. Eight kilometres, that was five miles . . . five miles to Strasbourg. They'd get the bastard yet.

Chapter Six

The situation had gotten out of hand. At first he had been scared. But after she had refused coffee and had asked for Kirsch brandy instead, he had begun to throw caution to the wind. After all, he had told himself, in a few hours' time he would be safely over the Rhine; the French would be fighting to take Strasbourg and the fact that he had had a 'dallianc' – he preferred that word to the other more drastic description of what he intended – would not matter one jot. Besides, it was clear that Gerda, as the blonde Hitler Maiden was called, was not the naïve innocent she had seemed at first. Obviously she had plenty of her father's bad blood running in her veins. Why, he would tell himself *afterwards*, she had actively provoked him.

He had taken her to his office in the *Kaiserpalast*. By now she was a little tipsy and giggled a lot. Most of the clerical staff had gone back to their billets and home and he felt safest there. The sentries guarding the HQ had other things on their minds than officers bringing in underage, tipsy girls, especially if those officers belonged to the dreaded Gestapo.

In the office he had opened a bottle of champagne and her blue eyes had lit up as she had heard the cork pop. "*Champus!*" she had cried in delight and had clapped her hands together, "I love *champus*." She had slumped back carelessly in the big, soft chair, her legs open, and he had been able to see right up her skinny legs to her virginal white knickers, as he thought of them. His head had reeled at the sight and he had downed his first glass of champagne swiftly, something she had copied.

The bottle had disappeared swiftly. By the time it had she was perched on his knee, his hand on her skinny white legs, as she giggled furiously. How beautiful and innocent she looks, he had told himself, though God knows how many men had already been up those short skirts. A child-whore that's what she was. A child-whore who deserved all she got. Why – she was asking for it, nuzzling his neck like that, with her legs thrown apart shamelessly.

He had opened another bottle. By now her eyes were glazed and this time she hadn't whooped with joy. All the same she drank the sparkling liquid dutifully enough, spilling quite a lot of it in the process. Then when that bottle was also finished, he had taken her brutally and violently on the office couch. She screamed and struggled, but he knew the screams and struggles were spurious. She was enjoying it, he knew that one hundred per cent.

Afterwards, she had not cried. Instead she had lain there, moaning softly as if he had hurt her physically, while he had gasped and panted. In a while he had put his hand between her skinny legs. The crevice was wet and hot. She was wanting it again, he told himself, like a bitch on heat. How corrupt and degenerate she was – and she wore the uniform of the Hitler Maidens! She simply had no shame whatsoever.

The thought excited him. He felt himself grow erect at the thought of her shameless needs. He had thrust himself into her once again, and she had wimpered and wriggled furiously. But he had held her down, gasping as he pumped himself into her savagely, "Now you little bitch, you're getting what you asked for – *and you like it too!*"

Then before he had collapsed, he remembered the change in her. She seemed to go mad with passion. She had bitten him savagely between mouthing vile obscenities, learned God knows where. And then suddenly she had arched her spine wildly so that for one dreadful moment he had thought she was having a fit. Right in the middle of his crazy thrusting, she had dug her nails cruelly into his fat buttocks, sobbing through gritted teeth, *"Oh shit! . . . shit! . . . I'm coming! . . ."*

Barsch awoke from his drunken, exhausted sleep with a start. A great hollow booming noise close by had startled him from his sleep. For a moment he could no identify it. Then he did. It came from Strasbourg's celebrated cathedral. He relaxed again, hearing her snoring softly next to him on the sofa. She was totally naked and he looked at her skinny body, with the slight, dark patch of hair at her loins, then covered her with his coat. He didn't want her to wake just now, for he was beginning to identify another noise besides that of the cathedral. It was the sound of muted gunfire in the distance. He sat up suddenly and wished next moment he hadn't. His head hurt like hell, as if two metal spikes were being forced through his skull to the backs of his eyes.

Next to him, she turned and her little white hand fell

on his flaccid organ. It felt good despite the hangover. He slipped his own hand between her legs. She was moist and for a moment he gently played with her. She sighed softly and stirred her buttocks. Hastily he drew his hand away, telling himself there was no time for that now. His life was at stake, there would be other child-whores once he was safe.

Hurriedly and silently he struggled into his uniform and boots. On the sofa the girl still snored. From outside came the soft tread of the sentries. Otherwise, Strasbourg slept, but there had been no mistaking that rumble of gunfire.

He buckled on his pistol belt and tiptoed out without looking back. She'd be whoring for the French in a matter of days, he told himself. A totally depraved child. Still, if he had had the time, he would have taught her some very pleasant things to do for him. Noiselessly he closed the door behind him and went softly down the blacked-out corridor.

In the hall next to the entrance, a helmeted military police NCO sat erect at the reception desk, a machine-pistol laid on top of it. Opposite, an officer snored at his desk. The NCO snapped to attention when he saw Barsch, who acknowledged the salute. "Is that the duty officer?" he snapped.

"Yes sir," the NCO answered apologetically.

Barsch tut-tutted. "Disgraceful behaviour, sleeping on duty. The man ought to be shot. No matter, when are my trucks due?"

Briskly the NCO looked down at the sheet of papers in front of him. "At zero five hundred, sir," he replied.

"Good! Then go over to the barracks and wake up

186

the cooks to feed the men. My escort can be woken, too. See if you can get those idle kitchen bulls to provide me with a cup of decent coffee, too. I'm sick of that ersatz muck."

"Yes sir." The NCO sped away like a shot.

Half an hour later his escort, fed and washed, assembled in the hall of the *Kaiserpalast*. All were 'old hares', men who had served on the Russian front with the SS and had been down-graded and sent to France due to wounds or illness. But they were a tough enough bunch, heavily armed and as aware as he was that the French would have no mercy on them after what they had done to the Maquis. "All right, soldiers, comrades," Barsch said hurried, keeping his gaze on the clock in the hall. "I won't waste time. Let's do our job and get on with it. Within two hours, God willing, I expect we shall be over the Rhine, and back home to mother," he added the soldier's expression.

There were grins at that.

"We shall work quickly —" the rest of his words were drowned by a sudden burst of heavy gunfire to the west. Dr Barsch's face blanched. That was the French all right, and it sounded as if they weren't too far off. He wasted no more time. "Everybody mount up immediately," he ordered urgently.

The men didn't need a second invitation. 'Old hares' that they were, they knew what the gunfire signified. Shouldering their weapons they filed outside to the waiting trucks, where the drivers were already gunning their engines, as if they couldn't get away fast enough.

Upstairs in Barsch's office the naked girl stirred uneasily in her sleep, perhaps subconsciously aware

187

of the gunfire. Then she turned on to her left side and fell back into a deep sleep once more . . .

Now in the grey dawn light, Mayne could see the squat outline of Strasbourg jutting up from the skyline of the great Alsatian city. Behind them Leclerc's artillery were still hammering away at some target or other, yet the sound seemingly had not alarmed the city's garrison. No sirens sounded, no tanks rumbled down its streets, no infantry were tumbling out of the suburbs to take up defensive positions. It was as if Strasbourg still slept, totally unaware of what was coming its way.

Paddy Mayne lowered his glasses and turned to Rory beside him, "Looks all clear to me, Rory."

"Yes. Either the garrison has already done a bunk over the Rhine, or they're just supply troops —" He stopped short.

"What is it?" Paddy asked sharply.

"Look. That side road at three o'clock."

Mayne looked in the direction indicated. A dark, muffled figure was pedalling hard on his cycle up a slight incline to where the side road joined the one they were on. A square bag bounced up and down on his hunched shoulders and he seemed to be wearing some kind of official-looking cap.

"It's a postman!" Mayne exclaimed, "A Frog postman, and the man we need at this very moment!"

"We need?" Rory echoed his words, puzzled.

"Yes, don't you see, Rory!" Mayne exclaimed loudly. "Who'd know his way around Strasbourg better than a postie. Just the chap we need at this moment." He turned to Stevens, the radio operator. "Stevie, nab him!"

Stevens gave that perfect smile of his. "With the greatest of pleasure, Boss."

Five minutes later they were on their way again, with a frightened French postman, suffering from a bad cold, perched in the fear seat of Paddy Mayne's jeep, alternately giving them directions and wiping his dripping red nose on the sleeve of his uniform jacket.

Now, finally, Strasbourg was coming to life. Men cycled to work with long loaves of bread tucked in their saddle bags. Little blue trams, bells jingling, headed for the factories. A column of German infantry, all unarmed, swung along lustily singing "*Oh Du Schoner Westerwald*" and before their officer could decide what action to take, the SAS had vanished around the next bend.

"*Cimitiere Central*," the postman announced, indicating the row after row of ornate graves to their right, as if it was important.

"Real old ray o' sunshine," Stevens commented.

Paddy Mayne wasn't listening. He said in the mixture of French and German he was using with the postman. "*Und jetzt . . . par ici?*"

The postman nodded and Stevens dodged quickly as a dewdrop from the civilian's nose came heading his way. "*Ja gerade aus . . . Boulevard du President Wilson.*"

Moments later they were crossing the main road which was part of the ring-road that ran round the city, when it happened.

A single shot rang out. Civilians on the pavements to left and right scattered madly. That single shot seemed to serve as a signal. For now a wild firing broke out from the green belt to their left and figures in camouflaged helmets and smocks were beginning to run forward, crouched low, but determined.

"That's frigging well gorn and torn it!" Stevens exclaimed in a sinking voice, for he had recognized the uniform at once.

So had the postman. "*SS*," he quavered and tried to bury himself in the body of the Jeep next to Stevens' feet as the driver swung the vehicle right onto the pavement, narrowly avoiding the terrified civilians lying there.

The battle had commenced.

Chapter Seven

The fat professor was the same as ever, although it was quite clear from the gunfire and the rumble of tanks passing the university, that the city would be under attack soon. He fussed over his precious collection, giving instructions to the SS escort, crying out in alarm if some of the embalming fluid escaped from the glass containers; mincing back and forth with them as if he couldn't trust his bizarre bits and pieces of human bodies out of his sight for one moment.

Watching the macabre scene, smoking and secretly drinking from the hip flask he had concealed in his tunic, Barsch would dearly like to kick the professor in his fat rump. But he knew he daren't do that. He needed him and his specimens to get him across the Rhine.

One of his men staggered by him bearing the case containing the pickled Jewish penis. He looked at Barsch and growled, "What a frigging life, being a porter for a Yiddish dick!"

Personally Barsch thought the same. Aloud, however, he snapped, "Get on with it, man. We haven't got much time left." He cocked his head to one side. "Can't you hear that? That's small arms fire. The Frogs are getting close."

That did it. Without another word, the 'Old Hare' hurried off with his "Yiddish dick".

The professor waddled up. He stank of sweat and formaldehyde. Barsch's already queasy stomach churned. But he forced himself to ask, as if he were concerned, which he was not, "And you, *Herr Professor*, what will you do?"

The professor spread his pudgy hands outwards. "I am not the least bit concerned, *mein lieber Barsch*. It is just a flash in the pan. Our brave German *landsers* will hold out here in Strasbourg, never fear. My only concern is to get the collection out," he said the word, as if it were in italics, "before trouble breaks out."

"I understand, *Herr Professor*," Barsch answered. "German science comes first and then we ordinary mortals."

"Exactly."

Barsch took out his 'Jewish tit', and filled some more tobacco into his pipe nervously, with a hand that trembled badly. The snap-and-crack of a fire fight seemed to be closer now. It was time to be off.

Now they were clearing out the last pieces of the fat professor's four-year collection and as he watched them being transported down the corridor he was obviously moved, for he removed his glasses and cleaned them, tears glinting in his crossed eyes. "Part of my life, Barsch, part of my life," he sighed sadly. "Thanks to you and your colleagues I have been able to —" he didn't end his sentence. Round him the hall trembled violently, like a stage backdrop, under the impact of heavy shells close by.

Barsch had had enough. He pulled his pipe out of his

mouth. "*Herr Professor*," he cried above the racket, "I must be going!"

"But my dear Barsch," the professor protested. "There is still the aborted gypsy foetus. You remember you sent it personally from Natzweiler last December as a sort of Christmas present for me. You can't leave such a perfect specimen of degenerate —"

But Barsch was already running down the corridor to join the trucks outside, leaving the fat professor to stare at his retreating back, his face a mirror of bewilderment as if he could not quite understand the world any more.

Rory O'Sullivan acted as he thought Paddy would have wanted him to. As usual he had been bringing up the rear of the convoy when the SS had launched their surprise attack from the green area. But whereas the rest of the regiment was pinned down unable to move backwards or forwards without suffering severe casualties, he was behind the cover of the bend. He made his decision as to his front a furious fire fight raged. "Are you game, Smithie, to try to get that bastard Barsch before he does a bunk?"

"You betcha, Boss," Smith answered excitedly.

"All right, we're moving out now. Reverse and keep your eyes skinned for these SS bastards."

"Like tinned tomatoes, Boss," Smith said cheerfully, as he started to reverse the Jeep.

Then they had turned and were advancing cautiously towards the *Gare Central*, where Rory knew a road branched off to the left, leading straight to the German HQ at the *Kaiserpalast*.

It seemed now that the great Alsatian city was waking up to the fact that it was under attack. Already German civilians, panicked and harassed, were heading for the station, lugging heavy suitcases with them, the women tugging at weeping, screaming, frightened little children.

The locals, who presumably had not sided with the Germans during their four-year stay in the city, were laughing and jeering at the fugitives, using French for the first time since 1940, yelling, *"Au voir, salauds"* and making threatening gestures with their fists. Here and there, snipers in upper floors were starting to take potshots at the Germans.

"Christ! What a mess, Boss," Smith commented contemptuously. "But it's allus the same with foreigners, they allus crack up in the frigging end and go to frigging pieces. Not like us!"

Despite his tension, Rory grinned. Smith was typical of his time and class. He'd escaped the dire poverty of the Depression in the North East by joining the Grenadier Guards and for years had risked his life for less than a pound a week. All the same, he felt the ordinary Englishman was ten times superior to the average foreigner. Yes, the Smiths of this world were the salt of the earth.

To the right of the station a group of young German soldiers, not one of them looking over 17, were attempting to set up a heavy machine-gun. When they saw the Jeep, they started to unsling their rifles. But Rory was quicker, he pressed the triggers of the twin K Vickers mounted at each side of the bonnet. A stream of bullets hurtled forward. The young soldiers jerked into violent action like dolls being worked by a

194

demented puppet master. Within seconds all of them were lying motionless or writhing in agony on the pavement. The Jeep rolled on.

They turned left. A German army truck had broken down and was blocking the street. Harassed German soldiers were attempting to get it started. They saw the lone Jeep and one of the Germans held up his arm like a traffic policeman in an attempt to stop them. Smith didn't give them a chance. He ran straight into the one with the arm raised, slammed him against the side of the truck, forcing it over, and next moment his foot pressed down hard on the accelerator, and they were racing down the street, zig-zagging from one side to another, followed by a wild burst of inaccurate fire.

Now they were passing big staff cars, filled with frightened officers obviously fleeing the city before it was too late. Rory nodded his approval. They were obviously heading in the right direction. Moments later he spotted the thin clouds of black smoke rising into the grey sky. He knew what they were, the headquarters were burning secret papers. In the desert when he had first fought under David Stirling, the founder of the SAS, he had seen staff officers burning papers only too often.

"We're getting there, Smithie!" he shouted above the clatter of a half-track, packed with soldiers going in the opposite direction, the men inside taking no notice of them; they were too intent in making their own escape.

"Let's hope that murdering Barsch geezer hasn't done a bunk yet," Smithie said grimly, clutching the wheel and concentrating on the panic-stricken traffic heading out of the city. "I'd dearly love to get my pinkies on him."

"You will," Rory assured him. "You will, Smithie!"

Dr Barsch was in the lead vehicle, followed by the little convoy bearing the fat academic's 'collection'. Traffic was getting ever thicker. There were not only trucks, but civilians and soldiers all trying to escape with their pathetic bits and pieces, laden on to horse, drawn carts, children's prams, bicycles – anything on wheels. Here and there both soldiers and civilians stood at the side of the crowded streets leading to the Rhine wringing their hands, the women in tears, begging the drivers of the trucks to take them with them.

Barsch had no compassion. "Run the swine down, driver!" he bellowed above the noise. "We have no time for them!"

"*Jawohl!*" his driver yelled back, for he was as scared as his master. For now the guns of the forts – Kleber, Foch, Petain – had begun to open fire, which made it quite clear that the French were on the outskirts of Strasbourg. They didn't have long now if they were going to make their escape before the city fell.

Now, the traffic was beginning to slow down even more. An angry, frightened frustrated Barsch swung himself out of the truck's cab and stood on the footplate. "What's going on?" he yelled to the group of soldiers in a horse-drawn cart stopped in front of his little convoy.

"Chaindogs," one of the soldiers yelled back. "They're stopping everybody without a proper pass to cross the Rhine. They're trying to form alarm companies."

Barsch cursed. It was the usual tactic in a retreat. The military police, known as the 'chaindogs', because of the silver chains and gorget round their neck and hanging on their chest, formed up companies of anyone capable of holding a rifle and marched them off to the front whether they wanted to go or not. The alternative was to be shot on the spot.

He slumped down in his seat for a moment. What was he to do? He had the authority to cross the Rhine. No chaindog dare question a document signed by the *Reichsführer SS* himself. But if he left the truck and pushed his way to where the MPs had set their barrier, he might well lose his little convoy and that 'collection' which was his ticket to safety in the chaotic confusion.

Damn, he raged to himself, it was an impossible situation. After all he had done to get this far, he was being stopped by a bunch of bone-headed chaindogs who thought they could stop a French armoured division with this demoralised rabble.

Smith hit the brakes. The Jeep skidded to a stop in front of the *Kaiserpalast*. A frightened soldier, standing guard still, raised his rifle. Rory was quicker on the draw. He fired from the hip as he sprang out of the Jeep. The sentry screamed and slammed face-forward to the cobbles, dead before he hit the ground. "Come on, Smithie!" Rory yelled. "Leave the engine running. This is going to be shoot and scoot!"

Smith needed no urging. He seized a tommy gun

from the back and bolted after Rory. All about them blackened shreds of paper came raining down, the secret papers which the staff had burned. They doubled into the big hall. A clerk still sat at the reception desk. Behind his glasses, his eyes looked dazed and uncomprehending. Rory could see why. There was an empty bottle of schnaps lying on its side in front of him and another stone bottle of the fiery liquid stood next to it. "*Wo . . . Doktor Barsch?*" Rory demanded in his broken German.

"*Oben*," the clerk managed to stutter. "*Zweite Etage . . .*" He reached for the stone bottle and took a hefty swig straight from the neck.

"Come on!" Rory yelled. "Second floor!"

Together they pelted up the massive staircase. Paper lay everywhere. There was also a leather briefcase bulging with official-looking documents, which someone had dropped in panic. For some reason there was a pair of frilly lacy knickers, too. "Somebody's gonna find it a bit chilly, Boss," Smith commented and grinned.

But Rory had no time to return the grin. As they swung into the corridor, boots clattering on the stone tiles, he searched frantically for the name of Dr Barsch on an office. An officer, chest heavy with decoration, came staggering down the corridor, swinging a bottle.

"*Nach mir die Sindflut*," he cried drunkenly and swayed so badly that he nearly fell over. "*Prosit, meine Herren!*" He raised the bottle in toast. Smith gave him a push and he fell over, to begin snoring almost at once.

They ran on.

"*Barsch*!" Rory exclaimed. "There – look!"

The two of them skidded to a halt. They raised their weapons. The only sound was the snoring of the drunken officer and their own harsh breathing. Outside, the gunfire continued. Rory nodded to Smith and the latter nodded back. He understood exactly what he had to do.

"*Now*!" Rory snapped.

Smith raised the heel of his heavy ammunition boot and slammed it against the door with all his strength. The door flew open. Rory burst inside, Colt at the ready. There was a scream. A half-naked girl, her skinny hands clasped to her breasts, came out of the other room, fear in her eyes.

"What in God's name —" Rory began.

"*Nicht schiessen*," the girl pleaded.

Rory's glance fell to the floor. There was another pair of knickers there, too. This time they were simple white cotton ones. Obviously they belonged to this girl – child would have been a better description. What had been going on here, he didn't know and he hadn't the time to find out. "*Wo – Doktor Barsch*?" he demanded in his primitive German.

The girl stared up at him, petrified with fear. She opened her mouth. Nothing came out. He realised that she was scared stiff of him. He could understand why. He hadn't washed or shaved for days and must look a frightening sight. Suddenly he remembered something. He reached in the top pocket of his battledress blouse. He pulled out the metal box which contained his 'emergency ration', a bar of chocolate. He offered it to the frightened, half-naked child.

"Chocolate," he said softly.

199

"*Schokolade!*" the girl breathed in awe, for she hadn't eaten chocolate for years. The fear went out of her blue eyes and she dropped her arms and accepted the little metal box. Now Rory could see the blue marks around her little pink nipples where they had been bitten. He hazarded a guess that that was the work of the missing Dr Barsch.

He repeated his question.

This time the girl was able to answer; she was no longer frightened of him. "*Die Universitat . . . dann der Rhein.*"

"*Der Rhein,*" Rory seized on the word eagerly. "*Wo?*"

"*Pont de Kehl . . . die Kehlerbrucke.*"

Rory waited no longer. "Come on, Smithie, we're going to cross the Rhine." He turned and flung a "*danke!*" over his shoulder to the girl, who was stroking the little metal box of chocolate as if it were a live thing. Then the two of them were pelting down the stairs towards the waiting Jeep.

Chapter Eight

Now the first French shells were landing in the Rhine, throwing up huge spouts of water on both sides of the Kehl Bridge. The mob of soldiers and civilians had panicked, running forward, screaming and shouting, trying to break through the cordon of helmeted military police. The flustered officer in charge raised his pistol and fired three urgent shots into the air, warning them off.

For a moment or two they backed away, but a sweating, frightened Barsch knew it would be only a short time before they tried again. He bit his bottom lip till the blood came. What in three devils' names was he going to do? He had been waiting here like this for half an hour now.

Again the French batteries on the outskirts opened fire. Once more the crowd ducked, screamed and shouted, as another salvo of shells howled out of the grey sky and slammed into the water. Huge gouts of water erupted under the impact and obscured the bridge for several anxious moments. Barsch was no military man, but he knew what the enemy was trying to do. The French were attempting to destroy the key bridge across the Rhine so that they could cut off the several thousand German troops in Strasbourg and prevent reinforcements crossing to help them.

The French wanted a quick, uncomplicated victory in the Alsatian capital. If no reinforcements could be sent across the river, the defenders of the forts would surrender without a fight. Again a salvo of 105mm shells slapped into the Rhine, making the great structure tremble and vibrate.

Dr Barsch made up his mind. It was the chaindogs who were stopping him crossing. So the chaindogs had to be eliminated. He turned and, still standing on the running board, yelled above the noise. "Each driver will remain at his wheel. The rest dismount and rally on me."

The 'old hares' looked at each other. Their puzzled looks seemed to say "what was the *Herr Doktor* up to?" But now Barsch knew exactly what he was going to do. In the end ruthlessness always paid off. Later who would know or care what he was about to do now.

A little reluctantly, his men came up to the lead truck. "All right," Barsch commanded, "unsling your weapons."

They did so.

"Release your safety catches," he ordered.

"What are we gonna do, *Hauptsturm*?" Klinger, one of the men who had been with him ever since he had been first posted to France, asked.

Barsch looked at him almost contemptuously. "What do you think, you great oaf? We're going to make those chaindogs get out of our way —" another tremendous salvo of shells straddled the bridge. Again it trembled violently and a few great stones plunged into the Rhine.

"Come on. Let's not waste any more time!" With

his pistol drawn he started to push his way through the panic-stricken throng of soldiers and civilians, many of them crying with fear.

A ring of middle-aged chaindogs, all armed with carbines and machine-pistols barred the way. Their officer saw Barsch and clicked to attention, but his hard face remained set and wary. Barsch could see he wasn't a man to frighten easily. "A problem?" he rasped.

"Yes, *you!*" Barsch snapped. "You're stopping me crossing and I am on a vital mission for the *Reichsführer SS*. I have a pass signed by him personally."

The chaindog remained unimpressed. "All passes are cancelled, sir," he replied stoutly, standing his ground. "Everyone who can hold a weapon is needed at the front. The enemy must be stopped. That's the army commander's order." The chaindog looked at Barsch's SS men, noting their tunics heavy with decorations and wound medals, and added, "We can use some old hares like your little lot, sir."

Barsch didn't hesitate, time was running out. In the distance he could hear the rumble of tanks. They could only be French. "We're coming through," he snarled, raising his pistol.

The chaindog looked hard at him, more surprised then scared. "Are you mad? This is a court-martial offence —"

Barsch fired. The big chaindog gave a thick, chesty grunt and staggered back, propelled by the impact at such close range. "What —" Thick blood welled from his mouth and he fell against his own barricade.

Barsch's old hares fired a volley over the chaindogs'

203

heads, but Barsch's shot had done the trick. They lowered their own weapons, staring at their dying officer, eyes full of disbelief, their spirit broken.

The mob waiting to cross the Rhine saw the way was almost free for them now. They surged forward, soldiers and civilians, and started pulling down the barricade, while the chaindogs stood by powerlessly and the rattle of tanks grew ever nearer.

"Back to the trucks," Barsch ordered, yelling above the chaotic racket as yet another salvo aimed at the key bridge landed, making it rock back and forth.

The men didn't need a second invitation. The bridge wouldn't last much longer. They pushed and shoved their way through the crazy throng – beating with their brass-shod rifle butts at those who were not quick enough in getting out of their way.

The drivers started to move forward again. A woman carrying a baby, tears streaming down her ashen face, lost her hold on the child. It disappeared under the wheels of the lead truck, its head smashed to bloody pulp. The woman fell to the ground, in faint or dead with shock. No one knew or cared. Now it was everyone for himself.

Barsch stood on the running board as his driver honked his horn, swearing furiously all the time, kicking and striking with his pistol at the terrified soldiers and civilians who attempted to cling to the truck. Behind him the other trucks were swamped by similar panic-stricken people. "Get out of my way you dogs," he cried, his face crimson with fury. "Do you want to live for ever! *Get out of my way!*"

The first French tank swung round the bend, its aerial swinging to and fro like a silver whip. Next to it the pennant of the *12 Cuirassiers* flew bravely. The driver brought the Sherman to a halt, instantly taking in that terrible scene.

"French! . . . *French tanks*!" the mob screeched, as the gunner swung the 10 ton turret round and prepared to fire.

Then the tank shuddered and lurched back on its bogeys as the 75mm cannon belched flame. A shell exploded in a blinding flash of angry red light. The truck behind Barsch's reeled as if struck by a giant fist and men fell out of it. The glass crates splintered and discharged their gruesome contents onto the road, hands, legs, all those loathsome bits and pieces of the human body which Barsch had collected so assiduously for the fat professor.

On the other side of the river, the engineer officer knew the time had come to blow the Kehl Bridge. He had just spotted the French tank and reasoned that there would be more of them soon. Undoubtedly they would attempt to rush the bridge and gain a foothole on German soil. If they succeeded, he knew what that would mean for him – summary execution. Every engineer officer in charge of a bridge across the Rhine these days knew his life would be forfeit if he lost 'his' bridge to the enemy. Hitler had given the order himself.

Swiftly, he rapped his orders and his men started to swarm under the bridge's lower structure checking the leads and the wires leading to the detonators, while he surveyed the other bank anxiously through his binoculars. The crowd milling about on the other side were obviously in a state of great panic. Some were still attempting to tear down the MPs' barricade,

205

others lay flat on the ground as the Sherman tank sent a vicious hail of white tracer over their heads. A truck lay on its side, burning furiously, others still tried to edge their way through the mob. There were dead and dying everywhere.

The engineer officer lowered his glasses and worried his bottom lip. Should he hang on a little longer? There were women and children among the throng on the French side; some of them might still make it across.

His sergeant, the man's broad face streaked with grease and sweat, doubled up to him and, without a salute, snapped above the noise drifting over from the other side. "All wires correctly fitted up, sir. Bridge ready for firing."

He positioned himself behind the first of the four detonators next to the engineer officer and waited his orders.

The engineer officer still hesitated. Now the first of the civilians and soldiers were pushing and jostling each other in their haste to escape, as the second Sherman appeared from a side street and commenced firing straight away. A few people came streaming across the bridge. Could he blow the bridge and sacrifice their lives? It was a damnable decision to have to make. At the detonator the sergeant looked up at him pointedly. His life might well be on the line as well if they lost the bridge to the Frogs. The engineer officer frowned. What the hell was he to do?

Barsch's driver slammed the bumper of the truck into the remaining section of the MP barricade to clear a way for himself. The steel girders gave a little, but not enough for him to pass through.

"Dammit, man!" Barsch shrieked, beside himself with fear. "Clear it away will you!"

With a crash of gears, the sweat running down his face, the driver reversed and then charged forward again. Behind, the canvas hood snapped open, splitting the glass containers. Again the ghastly bits and pieces of human bodies flopped to the ground. The truck slammed into the remaining barricade once again and the girders gave a little more. But still the gap was not wide enough for them to pass through. Behind them yet another truck was hit by fire from the two Shermans.

"Just force the truck through!" Barsch yelled.

"We'll get stuck and the clock'll really be in the piss pot," the driver yelled back. Again he reversed.

Barsch had had enough. He dropped from the cab in the very same instant that Rory O'Sullivan's Jeep careered around the corner and the young officer spotted the Gestapo convoy, most of it now shattered and burning from the tankfire. Smith pressed down hard on the accelerator, twisting the wheel back and forth, weaving the little vehicle in and out of the panicking crowd before the bridge. But even as he concentrated on his driving, his gaze took in the scene on the far bank.

He could see the engineers running back and forth, carrying yet more crates of explosive, and the man with the flag and little trumpet which would signal that an explosion was about to take place.

"*They're gonna blow the sod,*" he yelled wildly.

"*Keep going!*" Rory ordered. They had come so far to find this swine Barsch. He was going to get him now.

They pulped the pickled arms and legs as they shot by the burning truck. Instinctively, Rory O'Sullivan knew that those who had driven the truck were the men he sought. He prepared for the one last action which would bring the long quest to an end.

They slammed into one of the SD men, the old hare Klinger whom Barsch had called a "great oaf". He yelled and went down on one knee, blood jetting in a bright red arc from his shattered leg. Rory's pistol flashed into his hand. Klinger looked up at him, helpless, fear written all over his ugly face. How many times had he been in the position that the Englishman was now. *He* had never shown any mercy, but he wrung his hands in the classic pose of supplication.

"*Nicht schiessen, Kamerad!*" he whined, tears of self-pity streaming down his cheeks – "*Bitte!*"

"*Doktor Barsch*," Rory demanded cocking the hammer. "*Wo?*"

Desperately, Klinger pointed to the barricade, where Barsch was attempting to clamber over a girder, while the driver tried yet once again.

"*Mit der Brille.*"

Rory understood the German. "The one with the glasses!" he yelled to Smith. "Come on, step on it!"

"But they're going to blow the bridge, Boss," Smith objected.

"Keep going, dammit," Rory snarled harshly.

Smith went on.

"Prepare to blow," the engineer officer ordered, his decision made. The first bunch of fugitives had cleared the bridge. A fat, bespectacled officer, running all out, arms working like pistons, was half-way

208

across. He'd make it, the engineer decided, if he kept going.

To his right the sergeant spat on the horny palms of his hands and took hold of the wooden plunger of the detonator box. Next to him the others turned their keys, which armed the boxes, and did the same. The engineer raised his hand and began counting off the seconds. *"One . . ."*

Rory sprang from the Jeep, which was blocked by the desperate SS driver's truck. He vaulted over the barricade and then he was pelting after Barsch, his legs covering the intervening distance at the tremendous rate.

"Sir . . . Boss they're going . . ."* Smith yelled desperately after him, as at the other side the engineer commanded, . . . *"three: BLOW!"*

The men at the detonators plunged home the wooden handles. Almost instantly angry blue and red sparks started to erupt underneath the bridge. Little puffs of white smoke burst through the cracks in the stone-work. The bridge began to sway and vibrate, the pace increasing by the second. There was a deep throaty rumbling. Now a sinister crackling was running the length of the Kehl Bridge.

With the last of his strength, his heart beating furiously as if to burst out of his rib cage, Barsch threw himself forward in one last desperate dive for safety, his ears full of that ominous cracking and rending.

Behind him, Rory felt the bridge giving beneath his feet. Now he was running like a drunken man, trying to keep his balance as the tarmac cracked and swayed, larger and larger holes appearing every second. Suddenly it happened.

There was a great all-enveloping roar that seemed to go on and on. In front of him the world disappeared into a scarlet, blinding maelstrom of intense light. He screamed. An excruciating pain shot through his body. Then all was darkness and he was falling . . . falling . . . falling . . .

Envoi

More O'Sullivans

Outside, the bells from the little Gothic church across the December countryside were still pealing their joyous notes. It was Christmas and although the news from the Western Front was bad – the Germans were attacking seemingly everywhere – Churchill had ordered the bells should be rung.

Lying in his hospital bed Rory O'Sullivan listened to them and wondered idly how the men were getting on. He had last heard of them being in Holland but on this Christmas Eve they could be anywhere. Knowing Paddy Mayne, he would ensure that what was left of the 1st SAS Regiment would be in the thick of the fighting.

Further down the long ward, filled with wounded officers, the young subaltern from the Coldstream Guards had begun to scream again. Any kind of noise seemed to set him off shrieking. It was probably due to the bells, Rory told himself. Poor young sod. The nurses and orderlies would be coming up soon with the straitjacket for him. The medics knew that he would unsettle the whole ward. All the young men with their shattered limbs and minds were just too sensitive. Already someone further down the ward was grumbling, "Oh, put a bloody sock in it, old chap. . . . Can't hear to think, you know!"

213

The swing doors opened. Rory thought this would be the RAMC chaps with the straitjacket. He frowned, it wasn't a pleasant sight to watch them tie up the young officer. Last time he had frothed at the mouth when they had done it. Then Rory's face lit up. "Well, as I live and breathe!" he exclaimed. "It's you, *Smithie!*"

Smith, his uniform immaculate, brasses sparkling as if he were just about to go on guard outside Buckingham Palace, snapped to attention and said very formally, "Good-morning, sir, good to see you, sir!"

Rory grinned and said, "Come off it, Smithie! When did you ever have any respect for an officer?"

Smith returned his grin a little uneasily and glanced down the ward to where the Coldstreamer was tossing and turning wildly in his bed. Then he cast a quick look at the cage above the spot where Rory's foot had been.

Rory followed his glance and said, "Don't worry, Smithie. They're going to let me grow another one."

"Me and the lads in the mob — " Smithie began lamely, but Rory waved him to stop.

"So they took my foot away to the ankle, Smithie. The medics tell me that they're going to fix me up with a wooden one." He hesitated and his cheerful smile vanished for a moment. "The question is whether Colonel Paddy will have me back."

Smith breathed a sigh of relief. "That's exactly why the C.O. sent me over to Blightly, sir. To pick up some reinforcements, to see you and tell you that even if you're down-graded to Grade C he'll have you back. He said he was never very good at paper shuffling.

214

You can become the 'adj' (he meant the adjutant), and do the paper shuffling for him."

"Thank God for that," Rory said. "I'll be out of this poxy hospital like a shot now that I know that." He could hear the heavy boots coming up the stairs outside. It would be the male orderlies with the straitjacket. Although the Christmas bells had ceased for a moment, the subaltern was still kicking up a racket. "What about you, Smithie? Are you going to get a bit of leave while you're here?"

"No Boss," Smith answered, relaxed at last. "We need all the bodies we can get in the mob, what with the Jerries buggering about like they are at the moment. I'm taking the draft from Victoria Station at midnight. Folkestone–Dover. All them kind-hearted ladies giving us bars o' chocolate and jars o' char."

"And nothing else?" Rory asked with a twinkle in his eyes. Suddenly he felt better than he had done since that fateful day on the bridge at Strasbourg.

"Well, I did manage to cock my leg over last night in the Big Smoke. Cost me a fiver – them Yanks have forced the frigging prices up – but . . ." He didn't finish his sentence, for the ward doors were flung open and two burly RAMC men with a white canvas straitjacket came hurrying in, but before the doors swung closed behind them, Rory O'Sullivan caught a quick glimpse of a young serious face which seemed very familiar. "I say," he asked, "Is that chap with you, Smithie?"

"Yessir." Suddenly Smith seemed strangely embarrassed. "I didn't know whether to bring him in or not."

"Wheel him in at the double, man," Rory cried as

215

the Coldstreamer began to shriek and scream as the RAMC attempted to pinion him.

"Miles!" Rory exclaimed, staring at the tall young man, still wearing the absurdly old-fashioned uniform of the Eton Cadet Corps.

"Hello, Uncle Rory. Colonel Mayne has agreed to take me," the boy blurted out, as if he felt that Rory might have some objection. "He said I can do my para training after the next op. I've talked with the Governor and he says. . ."

Watching them, Sergeant Smith remembered how Rory O'Sullivan had been back in the desert on that Christmas Eve of 1941*. Now he was a cripple like so many of the others in this ward. Would this next O'Sullivan end up that way too?

They were taking out the crazy officer now and Rory was saying, "We go through a lot of bloody O'Sullivans in the SAS, Miles, so you'd better watch your back."

"I will Uncle Rory, never fear," the boy said enthusiastically. "Gosh, what a privilege to join the regiment! It doesn't matter a a fig that I'm not to be commissioned just yet."

Outside on the stairs the crazy officer was yelling at the top of his voice, "I'll shoot any man who abandons his post. . . . Get back there, *or I'll shoot!*"

Smith looked sharply at the young O'Sullivan to see whether the shrieking was having any effect upon him. If it was, nothing showed on his skinny face. Smith told himself that young Miles O'Sullivan would be like the rest of his family: tough, hard, unyielding, doing

* See *Kill Rommel* for further details.

216

his duty for the Old Country and the King Emperor until it was his time for the chop. He cleared his throat.

Rory O'Sullivan looked across at him. "Is it time Smithie?"

Smith clicked to attention and, mindful of the other officers in the ward listening, snapped, "'Fraid it is, sir!"

Rory reached out his hand.

Smith looked a little shocked but he accepted it all the same. "Look after yourself, Smithie. Give my best to all in the Regiment. Tell Colonel Paddy I'll rejoin as soon as I can. We've still got to get that sadistic Barsch, remember, Smithie."

"Yessir!"

Rory O'Sullivan took a last look at his nephew and said, feeling suddenly very old, "Remember you're an O'Sullivan . . . of the SAS . . . make a good soldier."

Then they were going and he was staring at their retreating backs in a mixture of sadness and hope. Outside the bells continued to peal their message of good will in a world where there was no good will. Softly, Rory O'Sullivan, DSO, MC and bar began to cry . . .